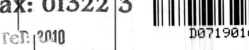
RHEA (NICHOLAS)
Constable along the
river-bank
(LA
=M+

Awarded for excellence
to Arts & Libraries

Kent
County
Council

CONSTABLE ALONG THE RIVER-BANK

As Constable Nick contemplates leaving the village in a bid for promotion, his wife begins her new job and doesn't want to leave their moorland home. Nick's constabulary duties continue, despite his personal dilemma – there is drama when children go missing and there is more alarm when a man disappears in the river. Cars also get stuck in the river and when Zachariah Isaac Pentecost (Zip for short) is taken ill, Nick discovers he has a long-lost son – but where is he? With Claude Jeremiah Greengrass causing his usual problems, it's all part of the daily routine for Constable Nick of Aidensfield.

CONSTABLE ALONG THE RIVER-BANK

Constable Along The River-Bank

by

Nicholas Rhea

Magna Large Print Books
Long Preston, North Yorkshire,
BD23 4ND, England.

British Library Cataloguing in Publication Data.

Rhea, Nicholas
    Constable along the river-bank.

    A catalogue record of this book is
    available from the British Library

    ISBN   0-7505-1978-9

First published in Great Britain in 2002 by Robert Hale Limited

Copyright © Nicholas Rhea 2002

Cover illustration © Barbara Walton by arrangement with
Robert Hale Ltd.

Published in Large Print 2003 by arrangement with
Robert Hale Limited

Magna Large Print is an imprint of Library Magna Books Ltd.

Printed and bound in Great Britain by
T.J. (International) Ltd., Cornwall, PL28 8RW

For William Simons
who in *Heartbeat* plays to perfection
PC Alf Ventress

Chapter 1

Arnold Merryweather, being a Yorkshire-man who was somewhat careful with his brass, always made full use of nature's resources whenever he wanted to valet his fleet of luxury coaches, or as others succinctly put it, to swill the muck off his pair of old buses. His bus-washing venue was a place called Hob Lane Wath, the site of a watersplash not far from Aidensfield Railway Station. There, a narrow country lane leaves the main carriageway to pass through the river and wend its way across the bleak landscape towards a couple of very isolated farms high on the moors. The watersplash, also known as a ford or a wath, lies just off the main carriageway and is easily visible to all who travel past the rail-way station.

The name of this ford is interesting because it harks to the moorland folklore of the fairly recent past. Years ago, during the seventeenth and eighteenth centuries, one of those remote farms – Hob Hall – was said to be the haunt of a hob. Hobs lived at various places on the moors, hence the name of several landscape features such as Hob Hill, Hob Beck, Hob Garth and, of course, Hob Lane Wath.

Hobs were said to be small, dwarf-like creatures not unlike goblins, who lived alone in the outbuildings of moorland farms. Described as secretive, ugly, bad-tempered little fellows covered in thick, shaggy brown hair, they disliked clothes and kept away from prying eyes. They worked day and night for the benefit of the farmer upon whose premises they lived, helping with essentials like the harvest and haytime and doing a range of other chores, mostly at night while the resident family slept. They were adept at turning hay, building stacks, ploughing, harrowing and thrashing, and also very heavy work which was beyond the scope of a mortal farmer working alone.

Not every moorland farm had a resident hob, however; it was only a privileged few who could boast such free and welcome expert help. Hobs worked with superhuman speed and strength and there is an account of one manhandling a loaded hay waggon the wheel of which had become firmly wedged between two rocks. The incident had happened late at night as the workers toiled to complete the urgent loading of the hay before nightfall, but the waggon's plight meant it had to be unloaded before its trapped wheel could be released. That would take a long time so the weary workers decided to leave the stricken waggon until morning when they were fresh and more able to cope with it – they'd get up early to deal with the problem ahead of the forthcoming day's work. But as they slept, the farm's resident hob came along and with his superhuman strength, released the waggon, took it to the stackyard and even unloaded it so that it was ready and waiting the following day.

Hobs wanted and expected nothing in return for their labours except a jug of fresh cream placed in the barn each night, but they were easily offended if people took them for granted or insulted them in any way.

One way of offending them was to try and spy on them as they worked, and another was to offer them clothes!

The North York Moors, a stunningly pretty part of Yorkshire close to the east coast, are rich with stories of hobs, such as the Hart Hall Hob of Glaisdale, Cross Hob of Lastingham, Hodge Hob of Bransdale, Hob of Hasty Bank, Dale Town Hob of Hawnby, the Goathland Hob of Howl Moor, the Scugdale Hob and one called Elphi who lived in Farndale. So far as Aidensfield was concerned, however, the Hob of Hob Hall was not so well known, but his name lives on in the name of Hob Lane – which leads to the farm where he lived – and also in that picturesque ford which crosses the river near Aidensfield Railway Station.

Wath is the local name for a watersplash. There are many such crossing places throughout the North York Moors, some with tarmac surfaces beneath the water and others comprising little more than stone blocks or even rough uncut stones, or at times, not even that! In some instances, waths comprise crossings over nothing more than the rocky bed of a stream, these seldom being used by modern traffic although in the fairly recent past they were regularly used by horse-drawn vehicles. These waths bear names like Blue Wath on Glaisdale High Moor, Birk Wath on Egton Moors, Slapewath near Goathland (slape is the local dialect word for slippery), Hob Hole Wath near Westerdale, Yoadwath near

12

Kirkbymoorside and many others.

For Arnold Merryweather, therefore, the ford known as Hob Lane Wath was highly convenient whenever he wanted to swill the accumulated grime from his precious coachwork. As often as necessary, Arnold would drive one or other of his purple and cream-coloured buses, either Bessie or Bertha, into the wath. He'd park in the running water and set about swilling away the dirt by liberal use of the river's flow aided by large brushes. To do this, he clad himself in fishermen's thigh-length waders and an all-embracing bright yellow water-proof cycling cape and an equally bright yellow sou'wester hat. He owned a splendid set of bus-washing brushes, one of which had a handle which could be extended to reach the upper regions beyond the windows or the darker regions beneath the carriagework, and even other nooks and crannies hidden beneath the vehicles where thick layers of mud tended to gather. Arnold also used buckets from which to throw water over some of the high portions, and a small foot-operated hose pipe which he could stand either in a bucket or on the river-bed, while a small ladder enabled him to cope with the loftier aspects of his work.

If his choice of clothing kept him dry, it also made him highly visible during his bus-washing operations, not that a bus parked in the middle of the river was difficult to see.

The sight of the sturdily built Arnold washing down either Bessie or Bertha was therefore a regular feature of life in Aidensfield and his efforts in the river brought a shine to their paintwork and set an example to others who had not cleaned their cars for months or even years. Bessie and Bertha were invariably very clean, the flow of the water being sufficient to carry away the larger pieces of caked mud and debris which were swept from their wheel arches or underparts during this operation.

I never heard anyone complain about Arnold emptying the ashtrays into the river or allowing oil to drip into the water and it seemed his small-scale industrial activities did not interfere with the wildlife or the resident fish population. Even during the summer months, the depth of water flowing across the ford was usually sufficient for him to achieve his purpose, although the winter, particularly with snow melting on the moors above, sometimes brought a heavy flow of fresh brown water into the river. This increased the depth and strengthened the flow, but it was usually something he could cope with. Certainly, a moderate rise in the water level did not unduly worry Arnold because it would take a mighty flood to dislodge the wheels of his buses, or sweep the vehicles downstream – indeed, the power of heavy water flowing beneath his wheel arches was an aid to his own efforts – although it must be said that Arnold himself was occasionally at risk of being swept away if he was daft enough to wash his buses in severe flood conditions.

If his waders filled with water, he'd be swept away like a bottle which would eventually fill to sink like a stone, never to be seen again. I think he knew that – which may be one reason he wore such brightly coloured bus-washing garments. If he was carried away on rising floodwaters, he'd be easy to spot from the banks of the river, or he might even be readily visible in the North Sea, should he be swept beyond the coastline without sinking.

During the time I was the village constable of Aidensfield, therefore, the sight of Arnold going about his bus-swilling routine was not considered unusual and indeed many vehicle owners emulated him.

Several farmers took their mud-encrusted

tractors and equally mud-encrusted cars down to the wath for a wash and brush-up and Claude Jeremiah Greengrass would occasionally venture into the water with his old truck to give it a cursory swill if he had some impending mission of a prestigious nature. I think he only washed his lorry when he hoped to impress the more important of his potential customers, but he seldom bothered to clean the interior because Alfred, his lurcher dog, would inevitably go for a swim and then leap into the cab to shake himself all over the seats and fascia. Among the others who made use of the wath were the coalman, who would wash the lower parts of his lorry, the milk-lorry driver who did likewise, and several other hauliers, ranging from furniture vans to cattle trucks; then from time to time, the owners of private cars would give their cars a quick swill in the river. Some preferred this to the prolonged hosing in the smart drives of their homes. The advantage of the river system meant that all the mud and dirty water was immediately dispersed, and it didn't get paddled into smart lounges, or on to freshly cleaned kitchen floors.

There was only one minor problem with this practice: from time to time, the two farmers, or members of their families and staff who lived on the moors at the distant end of Hob Lane, journeyed down to the village, usually by tractor, and wanted to cross the ford whilst someone was washing a vehicle. This was a fairly rare occurrence, however – almost as rare as those who wanted to visit those remote farms – but if it did happen, there was no aggravation. I was never approached to prevent vehicles obstructing the watery highway! The washer simply drove his vehicle out of the way to allow the other to continue his journey.

In spite of its merits, I did not take advantage of this free and natural car-washing facility either for my official police Mini-van or my private car, preferring to use a more conventional hose-pipe, brush and washleather. Another factor was that the small wheels of the police Mini-van, and the proximity of its chassis to the ground suggested it was quite possible that waves of river water could easily splash into the interior. I knew this would cause problems, to say nothing of the queries which would be raised by the official mechanics at Force headquarters when they serviced the van and found pools of smelly dampness beneath the interior mats. For this reason alone, I was one of quite a number of Aidensfielders who never washed my vehicles in the river.

But one day a newcomer to the village spotted Arnold washing his bus and thought it was a wonderful idea. He decided to make use of Hob Lane Wath. His name was Cranleigh Fotheringay and he hailed from somewhere in Sussex, his employers having transferred him to the culturally bereft northern regions of England where he worked in a plastics factory near Scarborough. I never discovered precisely what he did at the factory, but I understand it was something highly artistic to do with the design of new kitchen products. I believe one of his major successes was a box for the storage of cheese in refrigerators. Having long nursed an ambition to live a rustic life, he had found a cottage in Aidensfield and had moved in earlier that year.

He lived alone, I learned, and it was obvious, the moment anyone set eyes on Cranleigh, that he was neither a northerner nor a natural countryman. His rather effeminate and colourful style of clothing, his flamboyant haircut, odd mincing gait and lisping voice all presented an instant image to the stolid moorfolk. Some felt he would have been better on the stage or a fashion show cat-walk, but he was a very decent fellow, utterly charming and liked by all, even if, as we discovered, his nature was not blessed with a very practical streak.

His mode of transport, in which he drove to work each day, was a bright red Austin Healey 3000 open tourer and it was fitted with a towbar; for his holidays and some-times at weekends, he would hitch a tiny caravan to his car and vanish over the horizon on some expedition or other. Neither before nor since have I seen such a small caravan and don't know whether it was especially made to his requirements or whether it was mass produced. It was the image of a conventional caravan, albeit in miniature, and it was undoubtedly ideal for a single person. Clearly, he loved it.

Unfortunately, Cranleigh decided to wash both his car and caravan in the river at Hob Lane Wath and he chose an early autumn Saturday for the task. The low-water levels of the summer had ended and now, with more rain on the heights and lots of fresh water draining from the land, the level of the river was quite high, although it had not risen enough to be considered a flood or even to cause concern to property owners.

Nonetheless, the river was full of fresh water which was flowing powerfully at a high rate of knots. As the local people would say, 'There's a lot o' fresh coming off t'moors.'

Unfortunately, I don't think Cranleigh realized that the river was flowing both faster, higher and more strongly than normal. It was a fine, sunny, mild September day and he drove down to the wath. I was later to learn that when he entered the water, he felt his Austin Healey shift ever so slightly as the surge of water hit it, and at that moment he realized the water was considerably deeper than he had thought. It came halfway up his car and began to seep through the doors, but by that stage he was already committed to crossing the beck. Having reached the point of no return, he drove on and his car emerged at the far side. It reached dry ground with water dripping from all manner of unexpected places but the caravan was still midstream.

At that unfortunate point, the car engine cut out because it was flooded with water and the Austin Healey came to a halt. The worrying sideways movements had ended because the car was clear of the water, but within a split second, the movements renewed and he realized his caravan was receiving the full force of the flow. The high water had risen against it and thrust its enormous volume and power against the side of the caravan to create a massive force and, within seconds, it was being swept downriver like a rubber dinghy. It began to float as it was lifted from the ground but, fortunately (in Cranleigh's opinion) it was still hitched to the car. Unable to drive the car any further due to its useless engine, Cranleigh panicked and leapt out to try and steady the caravan with his bare hands, but it was a sad and futile action in the circumstances.

The power of the water was shifting the caravan as easily as a cork in a waterfall and it began to sway backwards and forwards, floating like a boat as the water lifted its wheels from the ground – and then it hit Cranleigh that, in his anxiety, he had forgotten to set the handbrake of the car. Quite literally, before his very eyes, the entire unit began to move, the caravan being forced downriver by the power of the water rising against its side and now dragging the car with it. Inevitably, as the caravan reached the edge of the ford, it was carried over and into the deeper water below while the car, still firmly linked to it, was compelled to follow.

As Cranleigh told me afterwards, he watched in total horror and with a feeling of absolute uselessness as his pride and joy was swept away to come to rest some thirty yards downstream. And there it stuck against some rocks with the water gushing and roaring around it, the caravan now lopsided and the interior of both being filled with filthy river water. Both vehicles had become firmly wedged against the underwater rocks and could go no further, but poor Cranleigh was now faced with the task of recovering the sodden pair.

Cranleigh came to report the matter to me, thinking there was some legal requirement to notify the police, but I could tell him he had no such obligation because this occurrence did not come within the definition of a road accident. There was no injury to anyone, and the only damage had been to Cranleigh's own property – and it was questionable whether they had been on a road at the time.

'So how did you get them out of the water?' I asked as he concluded his tale.

'I was on the point of contacting Bernie Scripps,' he told me. 'I thought he might be able to drag them out with his breakdown truck, but then a farmer arrived with a tractor and trailer, and he had a pair of long waders and a chain in his trailer. It didn't take him long, the caravan had become unhitched in the water and he fastened the chain to the draw bar and dragged it out in no time, then he hauled my car out. They're not badly damaged, apart from what the water's done to them, which will take some time to dry out and put right. I said I wanted to give the farmer something for his trouble, but he wouldn't hear of it.'

'Who was he?' I asked.

'I didn't catch his name, he was a small man with lots of brown hair and said he lived at a farm way up on the moors beyond the wath, something Hall, I think he called it,' Cranleigh told me.

'It would be one of the hobs,' I laughed, thinking Cranleigh would know that piece of folklore.

The incident concluded with no mechanical damage or lasting harm to the bodywork of Cranleigh's vehicles, although most of us felt sorry for him due to the smelly mess the water had caused. I understand his insurance company was very sympathetic too, but his experience made others reconsider the merits of washing their cars in Hob

Lane Wath. It made no difference to Arnold Merryweather however. He continued to swill both Bessie and Bertha in the river – it would take a tidal wave to wash them away, although Arnold might be considered at risk.

It was a few weeks later when I heard that Cranleigh had told people in the village that he had been rescued by one of the Hobs from Hob Hall. It transpired he'd thought 'Hob' was the surname of the farmer who'd come to his assistance, and no one enlightened him. That's how myths and legends are perpetuated.

Chapter 2

The comparatively simple recovery of Cranleigh Fotheringay's car and caravan was in direct contrast to a similar operation involving a Morris Minor belonging to a pair of twin sisters. Unmarried, they were the Misses Manners, Prudence and Priscilla, and their true age was one of the great unsolved mysteries of Aidensfield. Informed opinion, however, suggested they were well into their nineties, the supposition being that few, even among the more elderly of the populace, could recall anyone older than the Misses Manners. Everyone was certain they'd lived in Aidensfield longer than anyone else and residents, now in their eighties, had childhood recollections of the Misses Manners and their parents coming to live at The Lodge. The twins had looked grown up for some years before the arrival of the twentieth century – but in the mind of a child of three or four, a teenager appears to be rather adult. The Misses Manners were not true Aidensfieldonians, of course, having only lived in the village for seventy years or so, but it was generally thought they had been born during the late 1870s. That was often given as one reason for a reluctance to abandon their Victorian appearance, and a similar reluctance to involve themselves with lesser mortals in the village.

Prudence and Priscilla had always lived in the same house. It had been the family home since their arrival and they had no need to seek paid employment. Their parents had left them financially well catered for, following which an aged aunt had left a wonderful legacy which consolidated their ability to live comfortably without any thought of working. It meant the sisters were able to enjoy the finer things in life such as a splendid house with antique furnishings, a housemaid to do the chores, a little motor car, a sherry or two before every meal and nice clothes in which to be seen and admired. If there was a downside to their existence, it was that their somewhat restricted lifestyle had denied them any opportunity for meeting and socializing with suitable young men, and so neither had courted or married.

Despite their Victorian upbringing and demeanour, the two ladies were otherwise

26

quite modern in their outlook, being delighted – since the death of their parents – to visit the village pub occasionally for a snack and a drink, to go to concerts and events in places as far afield as Scarborough, York and Harrogate, to own and drive a motor car, to enjoy watching television programmes and to take part in many worthy activities both in the village and elsewhere. Not wishing to lower their standards, they had once been joint president of the Women's Institute, for example, as well as members of the parish council, governors of the primary school, trustees of the village hall and, for a time before reaching retirement age, Justices of the Peace for the Ashfordly Petty Sessional Division.

As they progressed steadily into their nineties with no apparent decline in their mental or physical prowess, they decided to relinquish all their formal activities such as committee work and voluntary help to others, in order to spend more time on their personal interests, one of which was painting water-colours of landscapes and wild life, including birds, animals and insects, their special love being flowers. In this they were unusual because both worked on the same picture – one twin would start the painting and the other would complete it, and it was impossible for anyone else to spot the join. I was to learn they'd done this kind of thing as children, in spite of admonitions by their governess, but even while being warned against such unacceptable practices, the girls had continued. In fact, they had carried on this curious method of painting well into adulthood, but with no thought of commercial success. For Prudence and Priscilla, it was a lovely hobby for them to share. Eventually, their work became much sought after by collectors and although the sisters maintained they had no desire to make money from their paintings, they were offered large sums for commissioned works – and they accepted. As their paintings became increasingly in demand, they were asked to increase their output and these new works commanded even higher prices. Quite unexpectedly, the sisters found themselves quite famous. For all their success, however, they would never paint unless they wanted to, having no real desire to earn money from what they regarded as a gift from God. For this reason, as life became rather too hectic with an increasing number of calls on their time, they restricted their output and produced only one or two paintings each year – which, of course, had the effect of making their work even more sought-after.

They continued to charge fees, if only to deter all but the most sincere commissions, and they gave most of their earnings to charity and throughout their lives, their distinctive style remained in great demand. I had seen some of their works in local exhibitions – their picture of an otter feasting on a captured salmon was brilliant and no one could see which half had been painted by which sister. Similarly, they'd done paintings of horses, all kinds of wild life, rustic scenes, seascapes, still life – and flowers. Flowers, particularly wild ones, were undoubtedly their favourite and they could paint a meadow full of buttercups or poppies, or a garden full of roses without anyone ever guessing it was the work of two people. Some experts refused to believe they shared the composition of every picture, thinking it was just a publicity gimmick. The ladies signed their work 'Manners' without any suggestion of forenames – thus only those familiar with their work knew that more than one artist had worked on the picture.

One morning in spring, therefore, Prudence and Priscilla decided they wanted to capture the brilliance of a river-side field which was full of fresh new daffodils. Wild daffodils grow in abundance throughout several dales within the North York Moors, Farndale in particular being renowned for its annual display. Glaisdale, Egton Bridge and a few other places also produce acres of wild daffodils, most of which are hidden from public gaze, while the spread along the river to the south of Aidensfield is another springtime delight. Near this point, there is a large, deep and brooding pool of slow-moving water where the downflow has eaten away the rock which forms the river-bank. The result is a dog-leg shaped bend in the river with a wood of deciduous trees above a low cliff which lies to the right of the pool as one faces downstream.

From that pool, the slow-moving water flows quietly then increases its pace as it rushes over rocks and through narrow gullies on its picturesque journey to the North Sea. On the other side of the pool, and continuing for almost a mile on the left as one faces downstream, there extends a series of open grassy fields. A footpath runs through them, linking one to the other like a thin brown ribbon, and by that route, it is possible to walk from Aidensfield to Crampton, a most pleasurable excursion at any time of the year. From time to time, I patrolled that footpath in uniform, performing a walking route between the two villages; at other times, of course, I walked it for purely leisure purposes.

In the spring, however, all those fields are full of small wild daffodils, now enjoying legal protection because of the silly and reckless habit of some visitors who dig up the bulbs and take them home in the hope the plants will flourish in a town garden – which, of course, they will not. That river-side area provides its own microclimate which is necessary if the flowers are to grow and reproduce themselves – unlike cultivated daffodils, these wild ones will not survive in suburban gardens. By digging up the plants, therefore, the thieves were effectively killing the daffodils. When the flowers are all in full bloom, that river-side scene is like a fairyland, with hosts of bright yellow heads bobbing and dancing in the gentle breeze which drifts off the water. With a scenic background formed by the river and the woodland behind, the daffodils were a perfect subject for a Manners landscape in water-colours. And so it was that

Priscilla and Prudence drove down to the river to commence their latest work.

Not far from the bridge at the foot of the village there is the entrance to a twisting and tortuous unsurfaced track which runs between two parallel dry-stone walls. It leads through the countryside above the river and provides access through a succession of gates to several fields which border it. Eventually, after about two miles, it emerges in Crampton. Despite its many bends and hills, it runs almost parallel with the footpath that passes through those same fields, but the lane permits farm vehicles to make the journey. It is also accessible to motor cars provided one drives very slowly with great caution, and with special consideration for the springs, exhaust pipe and anything else which might suffer from the rugged surface.

Priscilla and Prudence, in their Morris Minor laden with their easels and painting equipment, along with a picnic hamper, spare clothes and shoes, drove carefully along the narrow lane. Their intention was to park in a position which would give them ready access to their chosen field along with their equipment, there to capture the wonders of that river-side carpet of brilliant yellow spring flowers. About midway along, there is a sharp bend which turns left, followed immediately by a short but quite steep climb which, after about fifty yards, levels out upon a small summit. On the peak of that summit, the lane widens slightly and it is just broad enough for a couple of tractors or two average-sized cars to pass one another, and it was there that Prudence and Priscilla decided to park.

By placing their car as close as possible to the dry-stone wall on their right, they left enough room to allow any other vehicle to pass. The hilltop site was ideal – they had a grandstand view of the field below, along with the river and the mass of daffodils, and from there they could decide upon a suitable place to pitch their easel and little canvas chairs. In fact, just at the other side of that same wall, within feet of their car, the field also rose to a matching height and they decided to station themselves on that elevated patch, at least during the initial stages of their preparatory work. It meant walking back down the slope of the track, for a short distance and entering the field through a gate which was standing open. It was not necessary to carry their equipment very far – they could simply pop it over the wall as they unloaded it. And so they did.

It took a while for them to get their easel erected and settled into an ideal position for painting accompanied by their lunch hamper and other paraphernalia, but by 10.30 they were beginning their work of art, a new Manners landscape – *Daffodils, River, Woodland and Field*. As they worked, a tractor towing a heavy trailer full of manure chugged slowly along the lane, coming from the same direction they had used during their arrival and when it approached their parked car, it slowed down as the driver inched past. There was sufficient space, but only just and the tractor driver managed to guide himself and his trailer safely past the Morris Minor. But something happened. I don't think any part of the trailer or its load touched the Morris, but as the tractor pulled away towards Crampton and vanished down the other side of that little hill, so the Morris began to move – backwards. Whether it was vibrations caused by the heavy tractor and its load, or whether some part of the tractor or trailer brushed the little car is something we will never know, but the trouble was that Prudence, who'd driven it, had forgotten to set the handbrake. Parked on that small piece of level ground, the little car had been happy to sit there as its owners went about their work, but something had caused it to shift ever so slightly; once it began to move, of course, its own weight added impetus and soon it was rolling backwards down the slope, silently and quite slowly at first. The two ladies, concentrating upon their work, had no idea this was happening, neither did the tractor driver who, by this stage, had disappeared towards Crampton.

The car bounced and rolled backwards down the bumpy lane, its wheels guided by the ruts in the surface until it was running rather like a tram on tramlines but there was a corner at the bottom. Whether, under normal circumstances, it would have been halted by the dry-stone wall at that corner is something I cannot answer – although I doubt if it would have demolished the sturdy wall – but there was a field gate at that corner and it was standing open. It was the very gate used by the Misses Manners and, as it had been open upon their arrival, they had left it in that position. It was perhaps unfortunate that a set of those tram-line type tracks led from the lane through that gate, and indeed, led further down the field towards the river, but so happened that the Morris chose that route. Thus, the rear wheels of the lovely little car were guided through the gateway and into the field, and then, still moving in silence, it started its journey down the field which sloped gently towards the river. By this stage, of course, it had increased its speed; then with nothing to halt or slow its progress apart from grass and daffodils, it accelerated as it headed inexorably towards the river-bank.

It was around this time that Prudence noticed her car on its perilous trip and although she shouted at it and ordered it to stop, it ignored her and there was no way that two ninety-year-old ladies could gallop fast enough to catch it, board it and bring it to a halt. The car, by now travelling at considerable speed, crushed its way through a patch of daffodils, reached the river-bank which stood some five feet above the water level, and hurtled off rather like a war plane being launched from an aircraft carrier. It landed boot first in the water where it came to a sudden halt with its front wheels resting mid-way up the river-bank. Even if its front portions were out of the water, however, the rear was under the surface and in this manner, it came to a dramatic halt. It was some minutes before Prudence and Priscilla arrived to gaze in awe at the spectacle.

Realizing it was impossible to drive it away from this peculiar position, they decided they must summon help and so Prudence, being the more forceful of the two, told Priscilla to remain behind and guard their stricken vehicle while she went for assistance. And, I understand, she told Priscilla not to waste time standing and staring at the car, but to continue painting with one eye on the car as she, Prudence, might take some considerable time. After all, it was quite a long walk to the village, particularly for a lady of advanced years however spritely she may appear to be.

And that is where I entered the story.

I was at the garage, filling the tank of the police Mini-van, when Prudence appeared on the horizon looking very flustered, and somewhat hot and bothered as she strode purposefully towards Aidensfield garage. As I completed my fill-up, operating the pump as was my practice instead of bothering Bernie, she called, 'Mr Rhea, Mr Rhea, I'm so glad I found you ... is Mr Scripps in?'

'He's inside, changing an exhaust; shall I get him for you? You look as though you need to sit down.'

'I am perfectly all right, thank you, Mr Rhea, but I do need help, I need to be towed out of the river.'

'That sounds like a job for Bernie, not me,' I smiled. 'I'll get him for you.'

As Miss Prudence gathered her breath on the forecourt, I went through to the rear of the garage where I found Bernie working beneath a car elevated on a ramp. 'An emergency for you, Bernie,' I shouted, above the noise he was making. 'A towing job by the sound of it. It's Miss Manners; that is, one of them.'

'Give me time to tighten the bolts on a couple of brackets, then this car'll be finished. I'll be with her in a couple of minutes.'

I returned and told her Bernie would be along in a moment, then asked about her problem. She explained with a distinct look of embarrassment, then said, 'Oh dear, I shouldn't have told you about not setting the handbrake, Mr Rhea...'

'If you weren't parked on a road, then it's not an offence,' I tried to reassure her. 'And so far as I am concerned, that access lane is not a road. So you needn't fret about breaking the law! Your priority is to get your car out of the river.'

By the time she'd explained her problem to me all over again, Bernie had joined us, wiping his hands on an oily rag, and he listened as Prudence repeated her tale yet again. Then, after establishing the precise location, he said, 'Well, yes, Miss Manners, I can come along. I'll get my breakdown truck now.'

'Do you need me?' I asked.

'Well, two sets of hands are always better than one, Nick,' he smiled. 'And I am on my own today...'

'Say no more!' I had no pressing engagements and thought I'd make myself useful. 'I'll give Miss Manners a lift back to her car.'

Minutes later, and after a very bumpy ride avoiding ruts, rocks and holes, I was parking the Mini-van on the very site she had chosen for her Morris Minor, and after hearing her tale, I made sure I set my own handbrake before disembarking to walk back down the slope to the gate. As I helped Miss Prudence down the rocky incline, trying to avoid stepping into the tram-line ruts in the surface, I could see how they had guided the wheels of her car into the field – and then saw the newly made twin tracks through the daffodils and the bonnet of the little car peeping over the rim of the riverbank. Miss Priscilla noticed our arrival and came to join us.

'Mr Scripps is coming out with his breakdown truck,' Prudence told her sister. 'And Mr Rhea has kindly given me a lift.'

As I left the sisters and pottered down to the river-bank, I could hear the sound of an approaching lorry and turned to see the familiar sight of Bernie's breakdown truck heading slowly along the lane.

As I made my way back up the field to the lane, he halted close to the gate where I saw him chatting with the sisters; he seemed to be shaking his head a good deal, I thought.

'It's no good, Nick,' he said, adopting a solemn expression. 'I can't get down to the river-bank, not with this truck. This lane's too narrow. Those walls aren't set far enough apart for me to manoeuvre my truck through that gate. I need a large arc as a turning place, and I just can't get it here. It might have been possible if my truck could bend in the middle, but it doesn't.'

'I could guide you,' I said. 'You could go backwards and forwards for short distances, turning all the time until you'd got the truck in a position to drive through the gate.'

'Even if I did that,' he said, 'which I don't think will be possible anyway, that gate is not wide enough to admit this truck. You'd get a tractor through but not anything as wide as my breakdown truck. And if I do get into the field, I've got to get out again, maybe with that Morris on board or towing it.'

'What about my van?' I suggested. 'Can we use that?'

'Well, yes, it would go through the gate all right, and it's small enough to be man-oeuvred into the right position in the lane, but it's only got a little engine, it won't have the power to haul that Morris up that river-bank.'

The twins were hovering nearby and listening to all this chatter, growing more concerned by the minute as the difficulties appeared to be developing into something insurmountable.

'You'll have to do something, Mr Scripps,' simpered Priscilla. 'We must have our car back, it's so important to us...'

'How about a tractor?' I suggested. 'One of the local farmers might turn out?'

'And if I call him, he'll expect me to pay him, Nick. There's not a lot of profit in towing folks out anyway, the profit comes in repairing the cars afterwards, so I'd rather get this job sorted out myself, now I've got this far.'

'Maybe you could approach this field through another field?' I suggested. 'All these river-side fields give access to their neighbours, so maybe you could get into one of them at some other point, and drive through to this one?'

'Now that sounds sensible,' he beamed. 'Yes, you could be right ... oh, but there's just one thing.'

'Which is?' I frowned.

'These gates were not made wide enough for breakdown trucks; they were made for horses and carts, so even if I managed to get into another field, I still couldn't pass from one to another.'

'So what you need,' I said, thinking aloud, 'is a powerful vehicle which can tow another one out of the river, but which is slim enough to pass through these gates?'

'Right,' he nodded furiously. 'And I've got one that'll do that ... now there's an idea ... I've used it before ... to tow folks out of snowdrifts, muddy paddocks and water-logged showfields and the like. Yes, Nick, I think you've given me an idea. Just wait here ... I'll be back in ten minutes.'

And without any further explanation, he hurried off, climbed aboard his breakdown truck and began to reverse the entire distance back to Aidensfield.

'He's not abandoned us, has he, Mr Rhea?' Prudence asked with some concern, as she realized Bernie was leaving.

'No, he's behaving like a gas fitter or a plumber,' I smiled. 'He's gone back to get the proper tools for the job!'

As we waited, I asked if I might look at the painting in progress upon their easel and was delighted to see the beginnings of their latest work – it wasn't filling half the paper as I might have expected, but already it was using the entire span. I had wondered if one sister painted one half and the second sister the other – but after the initial faint wash for the blue of the sky and the green of the field, I realized Priscilla had begun to form the strong full background by making use of the entire paper. I could see that the daffodils would be the last things to appear in the picture ... so perhaps Prudence would do those?

As I chatted to them, I heard the sound of another vehicle approaching from Aidensfield and realized it was making its way through the string of fields. It was not the low growl of a lorry or the chug-chug of a tractor, but more of a purring sound and then, as I craned my neck to see the on-

43

coming vehicle, I realized it was Bernie's hearse. His splendidly polished but very ancient black Rolls Royce, with acres of shining chrome, was making its stately way towards us, its huge spoked wheels and high ground clearance making easy work of the uneven terrain while its standard car-sized width allowed it to pass freely through the narrow gates.

'Good heavens, Mr Rhea,' cried Prudence. 'He's bringing his hearse ... I do hope that is not some kind of omen ... things are not quite as bad as that, are they?'

'No, I'm sure they're not! It's one of the few powerful vehicles that will pass through those gates.' I tried to explain Bernie's reasoning. 'He said he'd used it before, to haul vehicles out of awkward places.'

'Well, I hope he succeeds without our little car having to go to its own graveyard,' smiled Prudence.

Bernie eased his gleaming pride-and-joy to a halt beside us and clambered out, looking rather incongruous in his overalls rather than his funeral suit, but he smiled and said, 'This will do the trick, she's never let me down yet,' and he patted the bonnet of his wonderful car. He went on to explain that the huge engine of the Rolls had all the strength and power he needed for most rescue operations while the massive wheels provided the necessary traction in even the most muddy or sandy of conditions and the high ground clearance meant the Rolls could cope with even the roughest of Yorkshire moorland terrain.

'She'll make short work of this Minor,' and he puffed out his chest with confidence.

Under the observant eyes of the Manners twins, Bernie reversed his hearse towards the river-bank and hitched a stout chain to the little car, fitting the other end to the towbar which had been discreetly fitted to the rear of the old Rolls.

'How can I help?' I asked, not seeing anything I could be usefully doing.

'Just stand by the Morris,' he said. 'Make sure the chain doesn't come off, shout for me to stop if you see summat going haywire. If things work out, she'll pull that little car out as clean as a whistle, and I expect it can be driven away ... the boot'll be a bit damp, I reckon, but nowt else. The engine's above water level, although the back brakes might need drying out ... anyroad, folks, let's get this job done.'

As the twins stood at a safe distance higher in the field, I stood by the Morris as Bernie hitched one car to the other, and then obeyed his request by standing nearby as he engaged bottom gear in his Rolls and let the chain take the strain. As the chain became taut, he maintained his pressure on the accelerator and surely but ever so slowly, the little Morris was eased out of his watery grave with water running from the boot and hauled up the steep river-bank into the field.

Before unhitching the dripping Morris, Bernie obtained the keys from Prudence and pressed the starter of the little car; it fired immediately and so, leaving the engine purring, he disconnected it from the hearse and drove it up the field, along the route it had already carved through the daffodils. He took it out on to the lane where he parked it near my Mini-van – there was enough space for both, one behind the other. Then he conducted a quick examination of the Morris, inside and out.

He returned and said, 'There we are, ladies, all done and dusted. No damage to your car, except some water in the boot. That'll smell a bit, but it'll dry out in time. Brakes are OK, they'll get you home all right – and I've set the handbrake this time! If you fetch it into my garage in a day or two's time, I'll give it a thorough check, just to be sure.'

'Thank you so much, Mr Scripps,' beamed Prudence. 'You have been so kind and thoughtful.'

'Think nothing of it. Well, I must be off. I'm supposed to be seeing a customer about now ... his granny's died and he wants me to do the funeral.'

'Honestly, I don't know how to thank you,' continued Prudence. 'Really, it was a remarkable display of ingenuity and care, Mr Scripps. A most commendable rescue. You'll send your invoice in due course?'

'I will, and pleased to be of service,' he smiled.

'Thanks, Bernie.' I was pleased he'd been so accommodating. 'Thanks for not giving up, others might not have bothered like you did. And that old Rolls – what a versatile old vehicle it is!'

'You're dead right!' he beamed. 'A right good investment, she is. And have I told you how I rescued that snowplough from a twenty-foot drift on the moor with her?'

'Er, no,' I had to admit.

'Or when the Territorial Army got that armoured car stuck in that ditch?'

'Er, no,' I admitted again.

'Or when Lord Ashfordly's horsebox got a wheel jammed in the cellar flap of the Hopbind Inn?'

'No, not that one either!' I laughed.

'Then remind me, one of those nights when you're in the pub,' he grinned.

'I will,' I promised. Minutes later he was heading back to the village. I turned to the twins and said, 'Well, that's a good job done. I'll leave you to your work now.

'Er, Mr Rhea, do you think Mr Scripps would object if we painted him into our picture?' asked Priscilla. 'With that lovely old car ... you know the sort of thing ... a busy working man with his lovely old car in a field full of wild flowers ... a most romantic setting I feel, and very apt ... it wouldn't be difficult to paint him in, we're at a very early stage of our picture and it would be a nice tribute.'

'I'm sure he would be delighted,' I assured them, although I must admit I wondered how anyone who viewed the painting would react to the image of an overall-clad man owning such a splendid old vehicle and parking it in the middle of a field full of wild flowers with trees and a river behind. They'd probably ascribe to the work some obscure social, political or psychological meaning

48

which was never intended by the artists; this picture might become a classic of the future, I thought, to be studied in art schools and universities for some deep and hidden message.

And all because an old lady failed to set her handbrake.

The rescue of the Morris Minor was not the only time I had to deal with an emergency in that stretch of river. The other occasion was during the chill of a mid-February morning, with frost in the air, ice on the roads and a layer of snow covering the moor tops. The snow was not lying deep but was just sufficient to provide a dusting of white upon the heights, rather like icing sugar on a dark cake.

The local people described it as a 'strinkling' – a delightfully descriptive word, I felt, somewhere between a sprinkling and a storm!

It was seven o'clock that Tuesday morning when my phone rang. I was on the point of waking after a late duty the previous evening, and the warmth of the bed, and of Mary's body beside me, could easily have persuaded me to remain under the covers. Beyond that cosy place, the world was cold, dark and unwelcoming and, as our hill-top police house did not boast the luxury of central heating, I was faced with a very cold start to my day.

I hurried downstairs in my dressing-gown and slippers, the chill of the morning making me shiver as I staggered towards the persistently ringing phone in my office. As I lifted the receiver, I realized the call was coming from a telephone kiosk – I heard Button A being pressed and the coin dropping noisily into its box.

'Aidensfield Police.' I was slightly out of breath due to my unexpected exertions. 'PC Rhea speaking.'

'Oh thank God, I thought you were never going to answer,' gasped a male voice. 'Look, you must hurry, there's a man in the river, that pool under the bridge–'

'In the river?' I repeated, rather stupidly.

'Yes! I think he's drowning otherwise I wouldn't have rung.'

'Right, I'll come right away ... can you return and do what you can till I get there?'

'Yes, but I can't swim which is why I called you.'

'I can; see you there!' I snapped, slamming down the receiver.

I knew the pool beneath Aidensfield

Bridge. It was very deep and deceptively calm on the surface, but underneath there were dangerous currents and concealed rocks – local fishermen were full of horror stories involving those rocks and currents. In this case, I wondered how on earth a man had managed to get himself into difficulties at this time of the morning, and at this time of the year. Within less than a minute I was on my way in the police van, reassured that among the vehicle's permanent cargo of emergency paraphernalia, there was an inflatable ring of the kind kept near swimming pools and harbours, and a long rope with a variety of uses, from towing motor vehicles to tying up stray animals by way of hauling the victims of drowning from wells and pools. I felt adequately equipped to cope with this disaster, provided I could get there in time. I was very aware that the caller would have had to run from the scene to the kiosk and make his call, then I had to respond and arrive at the scene. All this took time, precious time, valuable lifesaving time. Literally, every minute counted, which was why I did not have the time to ring anyone else. In very cold weather, of course, a person could survive underwater for a considerable period and so, even though it took me several desperate minutes to gather myself together and reach the scene, I was aware that a life might be saved.

Racing towards the river as dawn was heralding the new day, but forgetting that the roads might be ice-covered, I arrived safely to see a middle-aged man standing on the bridge. He was staring anxiously into the water, but turned and came towards me as I drew the van to a halt. I leapt out and ran towards him.

'Where is he?' I gasped – I was out of breath even though I'd come in the van!

'He's not here!' The man opened his arms in a gesture of defeat. 'He's gone. While I was ringing you. God, I wish I could swim... I could have saved him...'

'I'm pleased you didn't go in, you might have become a casualty yourself,' I heard myself warn him. 'That water is treacherous, and in this weather it's icily cold. Apart from that, if you don't know how to cope with a drowning man, he could have pulled you under the surface, or you might have been trapped by weeds or something. In the circumstances, you did the right thing.'

I was recalling the life-saving lessons I'd received during my initial training course and knew it was futile to leap into that water at this stage to carry out a search for someone who might be trapped underneath or swept a long way downstream – or not be there at all. I needed more than this man's eye-witness account. I scanned the river-banks for signs of the victim's presence – clothes, shoes, a cycle or car, binoculars, camera – anything which might have reassured me that someone had been here. Although it was not yet completely light I could see fairly well but found nothing; the river itself told me nothing either. The water, especially near the banks, was fairly clear and even in the poor light I could see, from my vantage point on the bridge, the bottom of the river where the flow was at its most shallow.

I could discern rocks and sand, some pieces of litter like beer bottles and jam jars, and in some areas, thick patches of green underwater weeds. In the deeper areas, though, I could see nothing, because the dark peaty colour acted to block any view of more than a few inches in depth, and the poor light did not help. It was impossible to determine by sight alone whether anyone was trapped down there.

I turned to address the man.

'When you rang me, you said there was a man in the river and you added, "I think he's drowning". Does that mean you weren't sure?'

'Well, I don't know.' He was about forty-five, I estimated, a small, nervous kind of man with thinning fair hair; he was dressed in a track suit and running shoes. 'I mean, he was in the water and shouting...'

'So what exactly did you see?' I put to him.

'I was out running.' He sighed heavily, as if the explanation was not going to be easy. 'I went along the river-bank – the footpath that goes to Crampton – and was on my way back when I saw him. I was down there,' and he pointed to the route of the footpath which I now could see quite easily. 'I heard splashing sounds and looked across the river; then I saw the man; he was splashing about in the water – out there, where it's deep.' He pointed to the area in question, then continued, 'I panicked. I must admit I'm not very good at emergencies, but I called to him and he shouted back and splashed about a lot, as if he was in trouble, so I ran to the kiosk and called you.'

'Was there anyone else with him? Was there a bike on the bank? A car?'

'No, at least I don't think so... I can't remember seeing anything or anybody.'

'So you left the scene and rang me?'

'Yes, I didn't know what else to do. I needed local help, fast, and thought if I dialled 999 it would take too long. He was in trouble. If only I could swim...'

'You did the right thing,' I tried again to reassure him. 'So can you describe him? What was he wearing, for example? Was he a poacher, or a fisherman, or a man walking a dog?'

'I don't think he had any clothes on.' He frowned as he tried to recollect the scene. 'I remember his arm was bare – the one he was waving – and he was moving about a lot and splashing. There was lots of water about which made it hard for me to see properly, and it was quite dark as well.'

'He sounds like a midnight swimmer to me!' I said. 'Except it's not midnight and it's the middle of winter. The point is what do we do next? I can swim, but there's no way I am going to leap into that pool not knowing for sure whether the man is there, and not knowing what's under the surface. It's impossible to know where to begin a search – he might have been swept downstream, too. And in that cold water without the necessary gear, I'd be a gonner in no time. We need a rubber boat of some kind, and police divers.'

'But that'll take a long time, won't it?' he pleaded. 'I mean, if he's still alive and down there...'

I looked at my watch. Already it was 7.30.

'You called me at seven,' I said. 'Allowing a couple of minutes for you to get to the kiosk and make the call, it means he's been missing for more than half an hour. Even in this cold weather, I doubt anyone could survive under water for this length of time – ten minutes, perhaps; thirty-five minutes, well, doubtful. But we will make a search, even if we're searching for dead body, not a living one.'

I had to admit to myself that I was not wholly convinced by his story. Certainly, he thought he'd seen a man in the water – but had it been a poacher, or a fisherman? He'd described the fellow as having a bare arm – indeed, he'd even said he thought the chap had no clothes at all – so would anyone go around naked at this time of the year? Even a potential suicide? In my view, his version of events needed clarification and substantiation, not a daring leap into the water even by one of our trained underwater search officers, or police frogmen as the Press were prone to describe them.

'Can I have your name and address?' I asked, notebook in hand. 'I may need you as a witness if we find a body down there.'

'Alan Elliott,' he said. 'I'm staying with my brother in Aidensfield, for a couple of weeks' holiday in Yorkshire. What a start!'

'Tim's brother?' I asked.

'Yes, he lives along the High Street, number 14.'

'I know him well.' Tim worked for an agricultural implement retailer in Ashfordly. He was a really decent man, a good cricketer and supporter of village events. 'Look, Alan, I needn't keep you hanging about here if you've things to do.'

'It is rather chilly, and it was a shock and Tim will be wondering what's happened to me.'

'OK, you go home. I'll radio for assistance and advice, and I'll let you know what happens.'

'Can I come back to see what you're doing? When I've got warmed up and some better clothes on, that is. I've only got running gear under this track suit, a vest and shorts.'

And so Alan Elliott trotted away as I

returned to my Mini-van and radioed Ashfordly Police Station. Alf Ventress, whose local knowledge of the district was unrivalled, was on duty and listened as I unfolded my story, ending it with a request that he alert Sergeant Craddock and call out the Underwater Search Unit to explore the river and determine the fate of the unknown swimmer. When I'd finished, he said, 'Nick, before we go into all that and launch a massive search, have you checked with Lawrie Dunwell?'

'Lawrie Dunwell?' I must have sounded completely baffled by this comment.

'Yes, the retired bank manager from Eltering. He lives in Aidensfield now. He moved there just before Christmas; one of those new bungalows just down the road from the church.'

'No, I haven't checked with him, Alf. Is there any reason why I should?'

'Well, yes, I would think so,' he said with confidence. 'He goes for a morning swim every day of the year, winter and summer alike, even if there's snow on the ground and ice on the water.'

'And would he do that in our river on a morning like this?'

'You bet he would! Even when he worked

in Eltering, where there is an indoor pool, he would go down to the river in mid-winter, or even to Scarborough for a swim in the sea. He tends to go there on Christmas Day, to Scarborough, I mean, for a dawn swim in the sea; he reckons it makes Christmas a bit special. He gets there and back before most of us have got out of bed.'

'I'll check right away,' I said.

'Right, and I'll delay those call-outs until I've heard from you – and don't go jumping into the river on some kind of bold rescue attempt. If I know Lawrie, he'll be at home now, tucking into his porridge, or whatever he has for breakfast, after an invigorating swim.'

I found Lawrie Dunwell's house and rang the bell. A lady answered. 'Mrs Dunwell?' I asked.

'Yes?' and I did not miss the look of concern on her face at the sight of a policeman on her doorstep at the crack of a winter's dawn.

'I'm PC Rhea, the village policeman,' I introduced myself, not having met her until now. 'Is your husband in?'

'Well, yes, er, well, you'd better come in.'

In the kitchen, I found Lawrie Dunwell, a tall, lithe and athletic man with a shock of fair hair and a skin that looked pink and baby-like. He looked the picture of health and was now dressed in a pair of slacks and a light sweater as he was finishing a cup of coffee while reading the *Daily Telegraph*.

'This is an unexpected surprise.' He smiled warmly as his wife hovered nervously in the background. 'So to what do I owe the presence of the constabulary at this time of day?'

'Did you go for a swim this morning?' I put to him. 'Under the bridge?'

'Yes, Constable, as a matter of fact I did. Is there a problem?'

I told him about Alan Elliott's reactions whereupon Mr Dunwell smiled and said, 'Oh dear, I do hope I haven't created too much alarm! I do remember a man calling out to me... I was just ending a delightful swim, Mr Rhea, and was thrashing about, covering myself with water to rinse off some of the mud I'd gathered, when that man came past, a jogger, I believe. He shouted something to me and I thought he was concerned about me, it's not everyday you see a silly old fool swimming in the river in winter, so I called back, saying "I'm all right", then he ran off and that was it. I left the river moments later and thought no

60

more about it.'

I did not tell Mr Dunwell that I'd almost instigated a search of the river for his body, but he assured me he would take more care to let worried people know that he was not in any kind of danger; in fact, he said, he'd been offered the use of an outdoor pool by a householder in Elsinby and was deciding whether to make use of that for his swims, midwinter or otherwise. Afterwards, I went to find Alan Elliott at his brother's house and explained things. He remembered the man shouting a response which was something like 'All right', but Alan had thought it was in reply to his call of 'I'll get help'. In fact, Dunwell had called out, 'I'm all right'.

I thanked Alan for his public spiritedness and later learned that Lawrie Dunwell had offered to teach Alan to swim in case he wanted to effect a rescue in similar circumstances on some future occasion.

But, wisely I thought, Alan declined.

Chapter 3

Most police officers, at some stage of their career, endeavour to map out their future. Not all are content to remain constables for their entire service; some are keen to progress as fast as they can to the highest possible position within their chosen profession – chief constable no less – although others seek only to advance into specialist departments, such as joining the plain clothes ranks of detectives or becoming drivers of sleek and fast-moving police cars.

The advantage of being a police officer in the 1960s was that after successfully completing one's probationary period of two years, the service offered what amounted to a variety of interesting careers. The CID, for example, offered promotion through the ranks from detective constable up to detective chief superintendent, perhaps with some officers spending short periods in uniform during the ascent of that particular ladder. It was thought that a spell in uniform broadened their experience, and it was also thought that a few years on the beat was essential for anyone seeking promotion, however specialized their role.

Within the Road Traffic Division there was interesting work for uniformed officers of every rank, some spending their entire career within the traffic department. In addition, there were many other specialized roles – Scenes of Crime, Scientific Support Services, Photography, Special Branch, Crime Prevention, Drugs, Fraud Investigation, Personnel Recruiting and Training, Finance and Administration, Prosecution, Complaints and Discipline, Firearms, Welfare, Communications, Community Liaison, Research and Development, Women Police, Juvenile Liaison, Police Dogs, Police Horses, Press and Public Relations and many others. Although, even in the 1960s, civilian employees were being recruited to fill some administrative posts, police officers continued to staff and administer many departments. In some instances, those specialized roles did not offer an entire career but were for the short term only, often being considered a useful stepping stone to higher promotion in some other area of work.

The precise nature of the specialized duties varied from Force to Force, but among the officers themselves, it was maintained that the purest form of policing was that undertaken by the uniformed constable on the beat. This work, the rock-like foundation of every police service in the country, embraced a huge range of experience whilst allowing officers to work closely with members of the public. The stimulus provided by this ever-varied work meant that many officers were quite content to abandon thoughts of promotion so they could continue to enjoy their duties. Many rural constables were of this ilk – they so enjoyed the freedom and personal responsibility of being a village constable in rural England that they had no wish to be promoted – promotion would mean a transfer away from such work. Sergeants did not perform the work of rural constables, although they supervised their work from offices in small towns – section stations as they were known. Each section comprised a small community surrounded by perhaps eight or ten rural beats; the sergeant worked in the town, eg Ashfordly, along with a complement of eight or ten town constables working shifts, while the rural beats surrounding the town each accommodated one constable. Each rural beat was centred upon a police house, and the bobby's area of responsibility could incorporate several villages around his own.

For a sergeant to be given the responsibility of running such a section, it was the usual practice for him, upon promotion, to work first in a more urban setting to gain a broader experience of that rank before being allocated his own section. Some of those section sergeants, as they were known, had no thoughts of higher promotion – being in charge of their own patch of England was all that they desired and in fact many extremely experienced officers, like Oscar Blaketon, were literally the backbone of the force.

Just as sergeants were required to have a very experienced background, often gained over several years before being put in charge of a section, so constables destined for rural beats were also expected to work for some years under supervision before being allocated their own patch. The essence of working one's own patch was that one should be reliable and able to work without supervision, and also have the ability to make one's own decisions and use initiative when and where necessary. It followed that a constable who was selected to work on a rural beat was often destined for further promotion, provided of course, he passed the necessary examinations and successfully performed his multifarious duties. Not many constables remained on rural beats for the duration of their service – although a few did – for most were promoted to serve, initially, as new sergeants in a town location.

Thoughts of this kind often dominated my mind as I found myself experiencing quiet spells while patrolling my beat. What was my own future?

Should I apply to appear before a promotion board? I had passed my exams some time ago, but the modern system placed the onus firmly upon the individual – those seeking promotion had to appear before a promotion board where they underwent a series of interviews by senior officers. The outcome of those interviews often determined the suitability of a candidate – but I asked myself if I really wanted to leave Aidensfield to become a sergeant working shifts in some local town with an inspector breathing down my neck?

If that happened, I knew it would not last for ever. Sergeants progressed too and were transferred from larger towns to smaller ones, often being the sole officer in charge.

In this way, therefore, I might eventually return as the section sergeant at Ashfordly – but that could not occur for some time. And if I succeeded in convincing a promotion board of my worthiness, perhaps I should consider a specialist post, even in the rank of constable? Such challenges and experiences were often very useful in paving the way to promotion.

Having discovered that life as a rural constable was so rewarding and satisfying, however, what should I do with the rest of my career? After all, I now had some twelve years' membership of the Force behind me – with only a further thirteen ahead if I wanted to retire with a small pension after twenty-five years' service. So, in effect, I was now at the half-way stage of my career – and still working as a constable. How far up the ladder did I wish to proceed? Certainly, I had no desire to become a chief constable or even a superintendent, my feeling being that such ranks meant that the holders had no real life of their own.

They were expected to socialize and play politics rather than function as a police officer at ground level. That sort of artificial lifestyle with its non-stop round of what amounted to compulsory socializing and attending formal functions along with interminable meetings was not my idea of happiness and contentment, so perhaps I had no ambition?

And then there was the question of the house. I lived in a police house. This was owned and maintained by the police authority and I paid neither rent nor rates. Thus I had no mortgage to worry about and so, although police pay was poor by comparison with others even in the public sector, I had the advantage of free accommodation. That was a massive bonus, but there were disadvantages. One was that I could be transferred, sometimes with only a few days' notice, to any other place within the North Riding of Yorkshire – and it meant my wife and children had to accompany me. So whilst a free house was an asset in many ways, it was also a liability. After all, the purpose of police houses was to facilitate the work of the constabulary and so those premises could not be occupied by wives and families only – they were there to enable operational officers to fulfil their duties.

However, the most desperate problem, in my view, would occur if I was killed or injured so severely that I was unable to continue as a police officer. Police officers were constantly open to such risks. An injury which halted my career would mean I would have to vacate my police house – and so would my family. And if I was killed on duty, my wife and family would have to leave, although there would be a suitable interim period for them to find alternative accommodation.

I must admit I worried about my wife and family in the event of that kind of disaster. What would happen to them? Where would they live? Would they be destined to spend their lives in a council house or rented accommodation? It might be argued that such thoughts and concerns were a mark of maturity for, as I advanced in years, my four children were also growing up and they required more money spending on them – clothes were important of course, as was a good home and a sound education – and it meant my salary as a constable would be stretched to its limit. So would promotion help? My salary would increase and that might enable my wife, Mary, to find life a little easier.

Promotion would therefore be of benefit to my family as well as myself, but at a personal level, I'd have to accept more

69

responsibility along with a dramatic change to my working life. Whilst I was supremely content at Aidensfield, I grew to realize that the future was hurtling towards me with ever-accelerating speed, and I suppose I began to consider furthering my career when I saw men younger than myself occupying positions of authority and status.

As each day passed, therefore, I knew I must soon make some decisions, the first of which was whether or not to appear before the next promotion board. If I did not, or if I failed to impress my superiors, I would remain a constable for the duration of my service. Even if that happened, there was no guarantee I'd remain the constable of Aidensfield until I retired and, on top of that, I knew I would have to vacate the police house sooner or later. Even if I stayed until retirement, I'd have to find somewhere else to live on a much reduced income.

As the weeks rolled past, I found myself thinking it would be wonderful to buy my own house. But on a police constable's salary? If I could achieve that, it *would* be security for my wife and family should I meet a premature end, but county police officers could not become home owners, could they? Besides, it would not be easy to get a mortgage based on the meagre pay of a constable in the 1960s, certainly not enough to buy a house large enough to be home to my growing family of four. One huge problem was that a constable who served in a county Force must be available for duty anywhere within the Force area; he had to be available for transfer at a moment's notice – 'in the exigencies of the service' as it was termed. Furthermore, all police officers' houses had to be approved by the chief constable, hence the practice of living in police-owned accommodation. In that way, transfers were comparatively easy for the authorities – officers were simply taken out of one house and plonked in another.

In contemplating promotion, there was much to consider, but being of a somewhat secretive nature, I tended to keep my thoughts to myself. I did not wish to put undue pressure upon Mary, my wife; she had enough to do, caring for the children and coping with my peculiar working hours. Certainly, Mary never put any pressure upon me so far as my future was concerned – dutifully, she looked after me, the children and the house and although I might have voiced some of my concerns to her, I was never aware of any nagging from her. Not once did she say I should be thinking of promotion or bettering myself; not once did she suggest we moved to a better house or to a town with more shops, schools and leisure facilities.

Perhaps I was lulled into a period of suspended time, thinking life would always be like it was at Aidensfield, but, of course, life is not like that. Life moves on, time passes rapidly and we all grow older and wiser...

And then, as we relaxed one evening before the fire, Mary broke the calmness of the moment by saying, 'Nick, I'm thinking of getting a job.'

'A job?' I cried. I wondered if I sounded angry, or upset, or both, but hoped for none of those. But I was surprised. 'What sort of a job?'

'It would have to be something that fitted in with school hours as I must consider the children,' she said softly. 'And then there's your duties. Neither of us operates on a nine-to-five routine.'

'So you're not talking of returning to your secretarial work?' I put to her. Mary was a qualified shorthand-typist who'd worked for the county council's education department and for local authorities such as urban district councils in areas where we had lived earlier.

'No, I couldn't do that, not with a family. I need something with flexible hours, where I can make my own working time. And I can drive. We have the car, so I could get around.'

'Are you saying we need the money?' was my next question. 'I know we're not exactly well off...'

'It's not that,' she interrupted. 'I can manage, but it would be nice to have a little extra sometimes. I think I need to get out more, meet other people, see more than these four walls and four grubby little faces at meal times.'

Mary was clever with her hands – she made all the girls' dresses and most of their other clothes, she made our curtains and settee covers, pillow cases and bedcovers, and she could knit sweaters for me and socks for the children and still find time do all the cooking and cleaning. I knew those contributions to the household were extremely valuable and her efforts (with my help whenever I could do so – I was fairly deft with a vacuum cleaner and yellow duster) enabled all six of us to live on my rather low police salary.

Certainly my income was limited and opportunities for paid overtime were scarce; if we worked extra hours for any reason, we were usually allowed time-off in lieu – a day and a half off for every eight hours' overtime we worked. The sergeant maintained over-time cards for each of us, totting up the hours until we could find time to take time off! Due to our shift patterns, rest days, holidays, court appearances and other duties, there was rarely an opportunity to take off the overtime which had accumulated. The Force preferred this system – they disliked paying money for overtime – consequently any such payments had to be justified, with signatures of approval on any application. Those signatures began with the local sergeant and went right up to the divisional superintendent, with questions all the way. Every signatory asked if the payment could be justified and in the unlikely event of the application reaching the finance depart-ment at Force headquarters, there would be further questions as to whether payment was justified. It was like getting blood out of a stone and it was very seldom such an application was approved. Payment was never easy to justify when our superiors ordered, 'Take time off in lieu'.

And, of course, being a police officer, I was not allowed take a spare-time job so that I could earn a little extra. Mary knew the multitude of restrictions upon my private life and she bore that cross with great fortitude. But now she was thinking about taking a job! I regarded that as a cry for help – my interpretation was that the family needed more money and it didn't require a genius to realize we would need yet more as our family grew older. As Mary sat before the fire after breaking her news, all my earlier concerns surfaced and I was now faced with the prospect of making a decision – *really* making a decision – about my future. But first, there was that job she was considering.

'So what sort of a job are you thinking about?' I asked.

'There's an advert in the *Gazette*.' I now saw that she had the paper at her side. 'Selling cosmetics. You need to have a car, to be able to work when most people are at home, and to have space to stock the orders. The commission is good, and there's expenses...'

'You mean you want to be an Avon Lady?' I put to her.

She nodded. 'Yes; I could earn a bit for myself, to help with some clothes or even a meal out occasionally, just you and me, and the children need more clothes now they are getting older. And it would get me out of the house and I'd meet people. I could arrange my hours to fit in with you and the children and the school.'

I could see that she had considered this option in some depth before presenting me with her idea and, of course, I had no desire to be obstructive if she really felt she wanted to sell cosmetics in this way.

It would enable her to meet people, too, and I knew she would be most discerning with her clients and customers, but deep down I could not dismiss my belief that she was really doing this because we needed more money. Quite suddenly, I felt as if I should be more assertive, more ambitious and more in control of my own destiny – and the only way, apart from leaving the police to take on some other better paid job, was to do my best to win promotion – and therefore to leave Aidensfield.

'If you really want to do that,' I heard myself says 'I'll support you in any way I can – baby-sitting, getting their teas, doing our meals, cleaning, or whatever. So what do you have to do next? About this job?'

'There's an address,' she said. 'I have to contact them for an application form and then I might have to attend an interview, that's if I'm suitable. I'll need a new suit for the interview, and for work, that's if I get the job of course.'

In this way, my world changed within minutes. Mary kissed me and thanked me for my support, then promptly set about her application to become an Avon Lady leaving me wondering about my own future in Aidensfield. The following day, a Wednesday, I was due to work a shift known as half-nights – 6 p.m. until 2 a.m.; the children were at school and Mary had gone to York to look at some smart new clothes in case she got an interview with Avon. It meant I had most of the day to myself, although I assured Mary I'd be able to collect the children from school – provided I wasn't called out to an emergency. She said she'd endeavour to return home in time to collect them just in case I was called out, but I said I'd do it if I could.

The snag with police work on a rural beat is that you never know when an emergency will demand your services – something as simple as a person calling at the house to say there's a traffic accident along the road required an instant response. I could not say I'd deal with it tomorrow, or even within the hour. Action had to be immediate. Even though we usually worked a set eight-hour day, we were expected to attend any emergency which occurred during our off-duty time – without extra payment, and then to adjust our hours if possible. I had intended to cut the lawn and do some gardening, but instead decided to take a river-side walk to think over all that had just happened. By doing that, it would avoid any likelihood of a call-out! If I wasn't at home, I couldn't be contacted. On this occasion, I did not want to be interrupted. I knew I must lose no time deciding whether or not to apply for the promotion board with all the consequences of so doing. Ultimately, it meant I must decide whether I was prepared to leave Aidensfield, or even seek a transfer to a specialist department. A long quiet walk beside the river would be just the time and occasion for me to concentrate my thoughts.

It was eleven when I embarked on my trip, suitably clad in warm trousers and a sweater plus a pair of hiking boots to cope with the muddy walk. Because there was no pub at

Crampton, I decided to head in the opposite direction, to Elsinby. I could have a pint and a sandwich at the Hopbind Inn, and be back home in good time to collect the children before my half-night shift. I left a note for Mary in case she returned before me, explaining where I'd gone – but not explaining why!

One of the paths leading to the river-bank led across some fields behind the pub in Aidensfield and so I opted for that one, knowing it would get me to Elsinby in about an hour and twenty minutes. But, as I climbed over the first stile, who should I encounter, also clad in walking gear, but my former sergeant, Oscar Blaketon, who was now the postmaster for Aidensfield.

'Ah, Nick!' He greeted me more like an old friend than a former colleague. 'Heading for some fresh air, I see?'

'I thought I'd stretch my legs,' I said. 'A hike to Elsinby and back, with a pint at the pub before I start duty tonight.'

'A good idea. I'm doing the same. It's Wednesday, my afternoon off, but Mrs Kennedy said she'd lock up for me at twelve, so I've got a good early start. I'm off to Elsinby too, for a pint and a sandwich. Care to join me?'

'Thanks, I'd love to, Sarge,' I responded with reference to his former rank, the habit of some years, but I wondered if I sounded enthusiastic. After all, I'd hoped for a quiet reflective walk on my own and now I had my former sergeant with me, no doubt with a fund of tales about the old times and criticisms of the new.

'I wanted some time alone; I need to think,' Blaketon said. 'But sometimes a burden shared is a burden halved, eh? So come along, I'll bend your ear if you don't mind, I need someone trustworthy to talk to. I've a big decision to make, Nick, and need someone to bounce it off.'

'It's funny you should say that,' I laughed. 'I wanted some thinking time as well, which is why I'm here. I might want to bounce ideas off you.'

'Well, if you want to bend my ear after I've bent yours, feel free. But you don't have to talk about it if you don't want. Right, Elsinby, here we come!'

Suddenly, the prospects of an interesting expedition grew more likely. We walked in silence for a while, each with our own deep thoughts, then Blaketon began to make comments about the wild life we encountered. He was identifying birds and flowers, pointing out badger routes and otter spraints, and then he said, 'Well, Nick, we're far enough away from the village and flapping ears for me to tell you what's on my mind. Shall I begin, or do you want to tell me what's bothering you? I can see you've got something on your mind; you've hardly spoken a word since we met.'

'No, you start. I can wait,' I said. 'We've all the way there and back to have our chat.'

'Right,' he said, and then lapsed into a long silence. I did not try to force him into continuing his narrative for I knew he was working out the best way to introduce his problem. 'Right,' he repeated. 'You know I didn't retire of my own free will?'

'Yes, you'd reached the age limit,' I agreed. 'All sergeants have to retire when they reach fifty-five. You had no option.'

'Right, but I was happy as the section sergeant at Ashfordly. I knew I'd never be promoted to inspector – I hadn't passed my exams for that rank – and I'd have been content to stay at Ashfordly for as long as I lived. But, as you know, when the system says you must go, then go you must.'

'I understand.' I could almost see my own problems mirrored in him.

'Housing's always difficult when you retire

from the police. I couldn't afford to buy a house and getting a mortgage at my age is nigh impossible. You can't save much on a police salary and there's no way I could have saved enough to buy a house outright – and so when the post office at Aidensfield was up for grabs, I thought it would solve my problem. There is a house with the shop – they, the house and shop, are both rented from Ashfordly Estate of course – but it was a means for me to find somewhere to live, and at the same time have a new occupation which would give me a few more pounds to spend, and something to occupy my time. With my rather modest savings, I could afford to buy the goodwill of the business and the stock at value, even if it meant renting the house and the shop.'

'I thought you'd done the right thing,' I muttered.

'It was right at the time,' he went on. 'And, remember, I had ten years to go before becoming an old-age pensioner, so I didn't want to be idle all that time. I had no intention of sitting on my backside to await the call of the grim reaper.'

'So the post office was a salvation of sorts?' I commented. 'Very timely.'

'It was. But it still means I haven't a house

to call my own even if I do have a nice little business.'

'But you're secure there, surely, even if it is rented?' I put to him.

'So long as I keep paying the rent, yes, but what happens when I want to retire at sixty-five? I'll have to sell the business and find another place to live. Lord Ashfordly's made it clear that the present premises will always be the post office so when I retire as post-master, the estate will want the premises for the newcomer.'

'It's rather like retiring from the police and vacating your house for the new occupier,' I commented, adding, 'So do I detect a feeling of slight unhappiness?'

'No, not really,' he said. 'I enjoy what I am doing, but I don't really feel fulfilled, to be absolutely honest. It's not very demanding, you must admit, selling postal orders, dealing with pensions and weighing overseas mail...'

'I'm sure there's more to it than that, Sarge,' I smiled. 'You make it all sound too easy. And you are doing a service to the public.'

'Yes, I am, but what I'm saying is that it's not the same as police work, not so interesting and lively; it's all very predictable. The one thing about police work is that you never know what's going to happen, even in the next five minutes. I miss that excitement, Nick, the buzz of activity, the anticipation of not knowing how you're going to spend your working day.'

'Are you telling me you want to leave the post office?' I decided to confront him with what I reckoned was his problem. 'Are you saying you need a gentle push from someone to help you make up your mind?'

He did not respond for some time and we circled the edge of a field, climbed a stile and found ourselves walking along the river-bank with the gentle ripple of the water to accompany us. The path was wide enough for us to walk side by side and after kicking a few reeds, throwing a stick into the water and pointing out a kingfisher, he continued.

'There's more to it than that, Nick,' he spoke quietly. 'And this is not for public consumption, not yet. I do have contacts, as you know, and some of them work for Ashfordly Estate – and I pop into the estate office from time to time, either to pay my rent, or to deal with some matter or other. It's a pleasant way for me to keep in touch.' He paused again, and I could see he was fighting to find the right words, or the right way of presenting those words to me. I did not respond, preferring to allow him to continue in his own time.

After a while, he went on, 'I've heard, on the proverbial grape vine, that Lord Ashfordly is selling some of his properties. Several cottages are to be sold; they're surplus to requirements, and he's going to put one farm – Throstle Nest – on the market. And he's selling the pub as well.'

'Pub?' I asked. 'I didn't know he had a pub!'

'The Brewers Arms,' be said, softly.

'In Aidensfield, you mean? That Brewers Arms?' I cried.

'That's the one,' he confirmed.

'But I thought it belonged to either a brewery, or that George Ward actually owned it?'

'No, George is the licensee, and he rents it from Ashfordly Estate. That was the system long before George took over. It's a straightforward rental – Ashfordly Estate gets no share of the profits, they just receive the annual rent.'

'So what's happening to George?' was my next question, wondering how Blaketon had knowledge I did not yet possess.

'He's not been well lately...'

'I knew that,' I nodded. 'He's been to see

the doctor and has had tests, a heart problem, I think.'

'Right. He's thinking of retiring. Ashfordly won't kick him out, he's been a very good tenant and has improved the pub, both structurally and from a trading point of view. But George wants to leave before he's too ill to work, even though he's only recently brought his niece over from Liverpool to learn the trade. You'll have seen her?'

'Georgina, Gina for short. Yes, she's been behind the bar recently. A lively young woman, eh?'

'She has no parents. They were killed in a traffic accident and George is her only relative – her dad's brother. She got into trouble with the police in Liverpool, nothing too serious. She was put on probation. George said he would look after her.'

'I knew that, Sarge,' I said. 'I don't think the villagers know, but it was a condition of her probation that she came to live with her uncle George. That's how she came to be here. But she seems to be fitting in very well, learning the business quickly and she gets on with the customers. In fact, I'm sure her presence is helping to fill the bar during the week – you can't beat a pretty face behind the bar to persuade male customers to come in! But it'll be a shame if George leaves; I've had no problems with him in charge, he keeps a good house and can maintain order. Just like his cousin George at the Hopbind. Good landlords, both!'

'The Brewers Arms is a good pub, Nick, a lovely handsome old building with lots of character, and a good reputation for its beer, and now with pubs going more into the idea of providing food, like bar snacks and even restaurant meals, I can see that we're heading for a big change in the way our pubs are managed, and the services they provide.'

'The breathalyser has made a big difference,' I said. 'Folks don't just go out for a drink, they want a meal with it.'

'Right,' he beamed. 'And pubs are adapting well, and, if you work hard, there's money to be made. I sense that we're at the start of an entirely new trend in the way we spend our leisure time. Pub meals, Nick, nice meals, I mean. Upmarket meals.'

At this point, I began to wonder why he was explaining all this to me, but his earlier reserve seemed to have melted and he was looking more confident, happy and sociable.

'So where's all this leading?' I asked, sensing that he wanted me to put a direct question to him. 'I can't see you really wanted to discuss George's future with me, or that of his niece, or the way that our pub culture is developing.'

He glanced at me and I detected just a hint of wickedness in his eyes as he said, 'I'm thinking of buying the pub.'

'Buying the pub?' I couldn't believe this. 'Are you serious, Sarge?'

'Why not?' He stopped now and stood with his hands behind his back, gazing across the river, and I realized we had a very good view of the Brewers Arms in the distance.

A fine building to be true and probably a very good investment, but a suitable purchase for a retired police sergeant? I halted at his side to enjoy the peace and tranquillity; I could hear the ripple of the river water in our moments of silence.

'There's no reason why you shouldn't.' I sounded a little hoarse now. 'It's just that it's come as something of a surprise!'

'It's not finalized,' he said. 'It's just a proposal at this stage, so I don't want any hint of this to leak out, certainly not to the villagers, and most certainly not to the constables of Ashfordly, not even Alf Ventress.'

'You are serious about this, aren't you?'

'I am,' he nodded. 'Very.'

I stood at his side and watched more water flow past as I waited for him to elaborate. I guessed he wanted to tell me more, and so he did. 'Like a lot of the aristocracy, Lord Ashfordly is hard up,' he told me. 'That's in the strictest confidence, Nick, which is why he is selling off some of his properties. He considered keeping the pub after George's retirement, and putting a manager in so he could claim a share of the profits, but that seldom works. A manager wouldn't have his heart in the business; you need a licensee who's going to work his or her socks off to earn money. Ashfordly knows that if he puts the rent up too much, no one will take it on, and he thinks the profits from placing a manager in charge would not be worth the effort, so he's decided to sell it. I happened to hear about it, in confidence, and, by a wonderful stroke of luck, my aged aunt Felicity died and left me a useful sum in stocks and shares.'

'How timely!' I felt a twinge of jealousy, even if I was happy for Blaketon.

'I regard that as an omen,' he continued. 'She didn't own a house but that legacy, with the sale of the goodwill of the post office, would enable me to buy the Brewers

Arms. I'd be the owner, not the licensee; I'd keep Gina on, certainly as barmaid and even as the licensee – her past shouldn't prevent her getting the licence – and I'd remain in the background, working on the books or whatever. I have seen the accounts, by the way, and they're in very good shape. There's a good living to be made, Nick. And since my wife left me, I get lonely living all alone – and you're never lonely in a pub! And then, when I want to retire at sixty-five, I could sell up and buy a small cottage somewhere, and have enough capital to invest to help eke out my police pension and my old-age pension. Or I could even stay at the pub and become a sleeping partner – there's lots of options, but the main consideration is that it's a form of security for me. You see, Nick, it would also mean I'd have a home of my own at last, even if it is a pub!'

'I don't know what to say, Sarge, except that it's a very exciting proposition, daring even, and you know I'll support you in whatever way I can.'

'You don't object to your former sergeant running a pub on your patch, then?'

'I don't object to *you* running a pub on my patch,' I smiled. 'I know you'll not give me a moment's cause for concern. I can't say the same about some former sergeants I know! But I wish you luck – it sounds like an opportunity which is too good to miss.'

'That's what I was hoping you'd say. Keep it under your hat until I confirm things, Nick. I wanted to chat it over with someone, to get their reaction, and I know I can trust you. So you don't think I'm too old to take it on?'

'Knowing you and your capacity for hard work, I'd say it was a wonderful idea, Sarge. You'll know how to pace yourself, you have a ready-made and very popular barmaid already in position and I know you'll make a huge success of it. Really, I do wish you every success.'

'There's a long way to go yet. We've got to consider George and his future, and then Lord Ashfordly finally has to confirm that he wants to dispose of the pub. Then there's the question of a sale price to include fitments, stock and so forth. It's all talk just now, with no firm commitments on either side, but I have first refusal. I've got the money and support from my bank and my spies assure me things will go ahead in the way I see them. I'm sure Lord Ashfordly will sell the pub and I'm equally sure he'll welcome me as the purchaser. And I'm not stupid, Nick. I know the risks involved and that hard work is necessary, and there's long working hours with lots of cleaning up and stroppy people to deal with – so what's new about that? Haven't I done that sort of thing all my working life anyway? And at least I'll be cosy and warm if the moors are covered with six feet of snow!'

'So if it all goes ahead, what sort of time-scale are you thinking about?' I put to him.

'Months rather than weeks,' he said. 'Five or six months at the earliest, probably a little longer.'

'Thanks,' I said. 'And thanks for trusting me with this news.'

'I'm pleased to get your reaction, but not a word to anyone, and not a hint of it while we're enjoying our pints in a few minutes from now,' he said.

'Scout's honour!' and I responded with the three-fingered salute of a boy scout.

'Right, onward we trudge then, and let me buy you a pint and a sandwich to celebrate, then you can tell me your news as I observe the way that a good pub is run – we never had any problems with the Hopbind at Elsinby, had we?'

'Not a scrap, Sarge!'

'And it's not Sarge any more. Call me Oscar, if you can bear it!'

'I might when we've had a pint or two!' I laughed, turning away from the river to complete the first half of our outing. Before long, we were sitting in a quiet corner of the Hopbind Inn at Elsinby, both taking care not to voice anything remotely connected with our earlier chat and Blaketon observing the routine of a country inn at lunchtime. The only comment he passed was that he felt some of the customers who'd ordered bar snacks might have been served a little more speedily, upon which I joked that if they had to wait a while, they'd buy more drinks to fill the time! And then it was time to walk home. Once clear of the village, and tramping back home along the river-side path, he said, 'Well, Nick. Over to you! What's on your mind?'

I must admit that by listening to his news, I'd almost obliterated the worries from my own mind, but he brought me back to reality and soon I was revealing the concerns which had dominated my mind over the past months.

I placed due emphasis on the need to make a decision about my own future while saying I had enjoyed – and was still enjoying

– my term at Aidensfield. I told him I'd be reluctant to leave and expressed a view that happiness and contentment might be more important than money and status. He listened intently, for I knew he must have agonized over the same dilemma in the early stages of his career and he reminded me that nothing was guaranteed, either in life or in the police service.

'There's no guarantee that even the most proficient and ambitious career constable will even reach the rank of sergeant,' he said. 'All sorts of factors come into play so what I'm really saying, Nick, is that you cannot guarantee your future no matter what happens and how you carefully you plan your moves.'

'I realize that,' I admitted. 'And I know there's insufficient vacancies for every qualified constable to get promoted; it's always something of a lottery which is one reason for opting to stay at Aidensfield without promotion. I happen to like it here.'

'But there's no guarantee you could do that either,' he smiled, gently. 'The normal term on a rural beat is five years; experience has shown that after five years or thereabouts, a resident constable can become rather stale and he may become too friendly with some of the people on his patch as well. It can reach the point where he is unable to function efficiently as a police constable, and so he is moved. And, remember, someone lower down the ladder might have caught the eyes of our superiors and he – or she – might be awaiting a rural beat ... your rural beat. If that happened, and you'd completed your allotted span of, say, five years, then you might be moved to make room for the newcomer. So where would they send you, Nick?'

'I've no idea,' I confessed.

'You'd be a constable who hasn't bothered to appear before a promotion board, someone not keen on bettering himself ... you could be shuffled aside somewhere, and forgotten.'

'A town beat somewhere?'

'Possibly. It could be anywhere, working shifts for the rest of your life. For all you love police work, Nick, I doubt if you'd like to return to that. You've done that already and now you've had experience on a country beat so the only way for you now, young man, is to keep moving forward and upward, not backwards or sideways. You've passed your exams – that was expected of you, you're very capable with words and

95

learning – and one reason for you being sent to Aidensfield was that you were seen as future material for advancement.'

'Crumbs, I wasn't really sure of that,' I said. 'It must look bad then, me not bothering to push myself forward.'

'You could always plead you wanted to be sure of your own skills before asking to appear before the board. But without passing the board, you've no real future. You could plod on here – it's a lovely beat and you're doing a good job – but where's it going to lead if you don't get yourself fully qualified for promotion? You're halfway there already, thanks to passing the exam.'

'I take your point,' I said. 'So if I do well before the board, I might be in line for a move leading to promotion?'

'You might, or you might find yourself being considered for one of the specialist posts – the crime prevention department, for example, something in community involvement or the training department – all good stepping stones, Nick, the way of opening doors. There is a big future for you, Nick, but away from Aidensfield. Aidensfield has given you a lot – and you've given a lot to Aidensfield, but nothing is for ever. You must, as they say, take the bull by the horns and forge ahead. But you need that record in your file, something to say you are fully qualified and, of course, very capable. And you just think of your family; you'll need more money to provide for them as they get older.'

'I think that message is clear enough!' I smiled.

'Now, there will be changes ahead,' he reminded me. 'There's talk of amalgamations of police forces, probably within the next few years, and that will mean more opportunities for promotion – and more town patrols around the clock for those who haven't got their exams passed. I might add, too, there is also a move to permit county police officers to buy their own houses. One or two have done so already, always with the proviso they'll transfer to another station if ordered to, but at least it provides a wonderful opportunity along with some added personal security. This is going to happen, Nick, I know it is, and I'm not talking rot. The early bird catches the worm, remember?'

'And it's all too late for you to benefit,' I sighed, feeling slightly sorry for him.

'Yes, it is, but I'm not complaining. Life was good to me and I was always happy at work, but it's not too late for you. Not if you start right now.'

'I get the message!' I said again.

'Good, so the minute you get home, fill in a Form 1 and ask to appear before the next promotion board. And if you fail, try again. If you pass the board, there's a whole host of goodies waiting for you, including a longer stay here at Aidensfield if you really want that, but if you fail, you could finish up walking the streets of downtown Middlesbrough, or coping with York's traffic and drunks on bank holidays. Remember the amalgamations are coming; remember there will be a chance for you to buy your own house; remember you need money for all that, and for your family, and remember that life never stands still.'

'Phew!' I issued a long sigh. 'That's telling me!'

By the time I returned home, I had made up my mind. I would apply to go before the next promotion board. After all, even if I convinced the board of my worthiness, there was no guarantee I'd be transferred from Aidensfield – or was there?

Chapter 4

Experienced police officers never under-estimate the importance of properly spelt and recorded personal names, one of their practices being to write the surname in capital letters. This is especially important when recording unusual names, names in foreign languages and those where there is little distinction between a surname and a forename, eg Robinson Readman. Robinson is a common English surname but it crops up surprisingly often as a forename as some families use their forebears' surnames as forenames for members of a new genera-tion. Sometimes these complete names are hyphenated to form a double-barrelled surname, but not always. John Robinson-Readman, or John Robinson Readman could be one example.

A person's name, however commonplace or rare, is extremely important, not only to the person who bears it but to others who have direct or even impersonal contact, and those who wish to identify the name-holder formerly. In spite of the multitudinous variety of names, it is odd just how apt are the names of some people. The person who taught me to drive was called Carr, while a local vicar was Priestley. A joiner in a village close to Aidensfield was called Carpenter; a local bank clerk was called Teller; and a lady in the haberdashery was Mrs Hankey. There was an undertaker called Boddy; a butcher called Butcher; an aviary owner called Starling; a cobbler called Footman; and a farmer called Cowman whose wife's maiden name was Bull. The landlord of the Green Man was called Brown; a barman was called Tippler; there were solicitors called Itchen and Scratchard; a slaughterman called Cattle; a kennelmaid at the local hunt called Fox; and a chip-shop proprietor called Fish. And I've never been sure whether there really was a firm of auctioneers called Gowan, Gowan and Gonn, or a police constable called Constable who was eventually promoted to become Inspector Constable. This kind of coincidence is fairly common and I am sure most of us can recite similar instances. Within police circles, the officers have an added form of identification, i.e. the number they carry on their shoulders or collars. In some smaller police forces in

100

the past, officers were referred to only by their number – eg 'You'll be supervising the Roxy dance hall tonight, Five,' or 'It's court usher duties for you this morning, Twelve.' More often than not, officers were addressed by both number and name, eg 'PC 575 Walker', or 'Sergeant 17 Smith', although inspectors and those enjoying higher ranks, did not retain their numbers. It follows that police recruiting departments around the country could have some fun matching names with numbers. I knew a constable called Walls who was allocated No. 4. Not surprisingly, everyone called him Four Walls. Similarly, when PC Goode joined the force, he was given No. 2, thus becoming Two Goode, and inevitably, Two Goode to be true. It's no surprise to know that PC Legge was given No. 11 so that everyone could confirm that Legge's Eleven, whilst a constable called Swallow was given No. 1, thus causing many to say that 'One swallow does not make a summer'. Constables bearing numbers like 999 or 100 or 1000 were always liable to be ribbed, and if a woman officer was given a number such as 36 or 38, it could be guaranteed that she'd be asked if it was associated with one of her more personal measurements.

It was while considering the purpose of numbers issued to police officers that a senior member of staff at police headquarters claimed they were unnecessary – he felt that the officers' initials alone would provide a form of additional and individual identification. When the force checked all their 1300 members, only two out of that number bore the same initials. Even the several John Smiths had different middle names and so his theory warranted further study – but nothing was done and the old system of collar numbers continues.

Members of the public tend to forget that they also have identification numbers – their National Insurance number is one example – but their names are most important – so much so that most can remember them! There are silly examples, of course, such those who name their offspring after television or film stars, or mindless football fans who burden their infants with the entire surnames of something like Manchester United football team. There are other thoughtless examples, too. I recall a family called Forward who named their daughter Eileen, another called Downe whose son was Ben, and yet another called Castle who named their son Windsor. Among the forenames given to people, one of the most unusual is Mahershalalhashbaz which, I am told, is to be found in the Bible and once I had to deal with a traffic accident in which the lady driver and passenger were both called Hypatia. Some families, especially those expecting to have lots of children, would begin the naming system with letter A for the first born, then working through the alphabet, Alan, Brian, Charles, Deidre, Eva, Frederick, although I've never known anyone complete the alphabet.

On the other hand, I have been told of a large family who used loosely sounding Latin names, the only ones I can recall being Una for 1, Sixtus for 6, Septimus for 7, Octavia for 8, and Decima for 10. I think there were thirteen or fourteen in that family, and I can only plead for parents to think carefully before burdening their children with daft names.

In many cases, though, a forename may run through a family with each eldest son or daughter being given that name down the generations. The male line of the Green-grass dynasty contained lots of Jeremiahs and in some of the more remote areas of the moors and dales, farmers with a history of Methodism in the family would perpetuate

Biblical names in their offspring, especially their sons, thus producing hosts of Aarons, Abels, Calebs, Enochs, Isaiahs, Reubens and the like. Girls in such families often bore names like Rachel, Naamah, Sarah and Rebecca or Rebekah. It is not surprising, therefore, that one of the older gentlemen living in Aidensfield was called Zachariah Isaac Pentecost, Zip or Zipper for short. Almost everyone knew him as Awd Zip and when referring to him, the locals would mention Awd Zip's house, Awd Zip's dog, Awd Zip's chicken run, or merely Awd Zip. Rarely was he referred to as Mr Pentecost. I thought this was something to do with the ancient navy-blue jerkin he wore because it had a massive zip which could be pulled up high about his neck – he was rarely seen without the garment. Later I wondered if his name was due to the fact he rarely spoke to anyone. As someone once said, 'Awd Zip's well named, he keeps his lips zipped up for most of the time.'

It was some time after my arrival at Aidensfield that I discovered Zip's pair of wonderful forenames. It happened in connection with another matter, when I was examining the electoral register to determine the name of a resident's house (few of the houses in Aidensfield bore name-plates). By chance I spotted Zip's name and discovered that the inhabitant of Woodford Intake had such a glorious and distinctive handle to his personality. I found this quite intriguing. Until then, I had never had cause to ponder his full name – if I ever found myself addressing him to his face, I called him Mr Pentecost, and on those occasions I might refer to him within the village for any reason, I found myself using his well-known local name of Awd Zip.

Zip's spacious home, which most of us referred to simply as Woodford, was a large stone-built house surrounded by lots of sheds and outbuildings, and it occupied a quiet position towards the lower end of Aidensfield, not far from the river. The land, which had been reclaimed from the lower reaches of neighbouring moorland, pro-vided a lovely site of several undulating acres, most of it highly fertile and ideal as a smallholding. There Zip kept hundreds or even thousands of hens, often with geese, turkeys and ducks among them, and he also maintained a few sheep, lambs and pigs and even half a dozen bullocks. He had a garden which was always rich with produce ranging from potatoes, carrots and beetroot to cabbages, lettuce and sprouts by way of soft fruit like strawberries, red and black currants and raspberries. He grew flowers too, and he sold his produce either at the gate, or to local retailers along with his other products such as eggs or dressed poultry. There was an orchard too, which, in the season, produced tons of apples, plums and pears. Awd Zip earned his living from this highly productive smallholding, usually displaying his produce on a table outside the gate along with a dish into which he expected customers to place their money without troubling him. Although he never made a fortune, the smallholding maintained him and his house. His needs were modest, however; he had no wife or family; he didn't run a car, or take holidays, nor did he venture to the pub for a drink or a meal, although he possessed an ancient tractor and equally ancient horsebox which he used to ferry his livestock from place to place. Being of rigid Methodist stock, he didn't gamble, drink alcohol, smoke cigarettes or attend social functions such as whist drives or Christmas parties, although he did support his local chapel both by his regular presence and by keeping it supplied with flowers. And when the harvest festival was held, he ensured it had a wonderful array of produce, most of it from his smallholding. His support for the chapel, and his regular visits on Sundays seemed to be his only excursion from home.

He did not seem to have any close friends or relatives in the area, and I gained the impression that Zip spent most of his time utterly alone – but it seemed that this was how he wanted to live. The village offered opportunities for him to socialize, but he rejected everything on offer by preferring to live alone in his fertile Garden of Eden, and never inviting anyone to visit him. Customers never got inside the house – and neither did any of his chapel-going associates. He always met them outside or in one of his outbuildings, or at the gate, and that included me and the local pastor.

I had very few occasions to call upon him, perhaps the only times being if he bought or sold a pig or bullock, when I would have to check and sign his stock movement register. But he never invited me inside, always preferring to do business on the doorstep, or perhaps in one of his sheds.

It was difficult to estimate his age. I thought he was well over seventy, probably nearing eighty. He was one of those countrymen whose appearance rarely changed with each passing year and in the time I knew him, he altered not one jot! This might be due to the fact he never bought new clothes, or kept pace with fashionable changes. During the whole time I had known him, he had worn the same overalls, jerkin and black boots, winter and summer alike. His weatherbeaten old face was always covered in three or four days' growth of beard. His grey hair, thick and lush with not a hint of a bald patch, always looked unkempt for I think he trimmed it himself and never washed it, letting the rain do that chore whenever he had to work outdoors in a downpour. With a pair of old horn-rimmed spectacles on his nose, he was a slightly built man with just a hint of a stoop. He was around five feet seven or eight inches tall and moved quickly in everything he did, darting from one job to another in much the same way as a busy mouse goes about its daily routine.

Having such a lonely life meant that Zip cared for himself at home, making all his own meals, caring for the house and doing routine chores like washing, bed-making and so forth. Certainly, no one from the village popped in to do his baking or washing, and he was not the sort of man to ask for any kind of assistance, let alone help with his domestic necessities.

As I spotted him darting along the village street to the shop or down to the chapel on Sundays, in the same clothes he wore during the week, there were times I felt he must have sometimes wanted a friend or companion but clearly, he'd lived all his life in a solitary manner, so who was I to expect him to change, even if he was getting older? And then one Tuesday morning, shortly after 9.30, I popped into the post office to buy some stamps, and found Oscar Blaketon chatting to the postman.

'Ah, Nick.' Blaketon broke off his conversation. 'Just the fellow. Jim says Zip's not around this morning, his curtains are still closed.'

'Is that unusual?' was my instinctive reaction.

'It's the first time I've come across it.' Jim Napier had been postman at Aidensfield for five or six years, sometimes sharing his round with Gilbert Kingston of Elsinby. 'Awd Zip's usually up and about soon after five.'

'Did you knock, or try to get him to come to the door?' I asked.

'No, you know what he's like, he doesn't like to think people are interfering with him and his life, or being nosy; he can be a crusty old sod at times. There was a letter for him, a circular of some kind by the look of it, and I put that through his box, so I didn't have to knock. His cat was outside as well, waiting to be fed, and all his hens were gathered at the wire gate; he usually feeds them early on.'

'What time was it when you called?' I asked.

'I first came past his house just after half-past seven, on my way into the village that was, and then I did my delivery to Woodford an hour later. Half-past eight or so. It was still all shut up both times.'

'Very late for Zip,' said Blaketon pointedly, and I recognized the attitude of my former sergeant. Blaketon was now thinking like a policeman and I knew I must respond – as I would have done anyway.

'Has he gone away?' I asked. 'Or been ill?'

'He never goes away,' Blaketon told me. 'And he's never ill. If he was, he wouldn't admit it; he'd not want a doctor or nurse within a million miles of him. He can be a cussed old codger to say the least.'

'I'll go and check,' I assured them, wondering what kind of reception I'd get from Awd Zip.

When I arrived, I parked outside his gate and walked the few yards to his back door, the one he always used. Yorkshire folk rarely use their front doors; certainly, a man who was always at work like Zip would never think of using the front. A white and ginger cat was waiting outside and it mewed as I approached, raising its tail in the air at the expectation of food. And I saw the hens, all gathered around the gate of their enclosure, clucking and pushing and shoving one another at the gate as I walked past. They'd not been shut in their henhouse last night but I doubted if a fox could breach Zip's stout wire fencing. As I grew nearer, I could see the kitchen curtains were closed, and then, looking aloft, saw that two of the upstairs windows displayed closed curtains. It was about quarter to ten.

Before attempting to rouse Zip or gain entry, I made a rapid tour of the outside of the house, partly to see if I could locate him through one of the downstairs windows, and partly to ascertain whether or not there'd been a forced entry. Where the curtains had not been closed, I was able to peer into some of the ground-floor rooms, all of

111

which looked tidy and neat except for one. I saw it had a toy train set arranged around the floor, and lots of childish things, photographs and pictures around the room. I wondered if the old man liked playing with trains in his lonely life. The rest of the house was tidy and filled with old-fashioned furniture. There was no sign of him, neither was there any indication of a forced entry. I had to see if my knocking would produce a result and so I first hammered on the back door, then the front, and then I rattled a few windows but gained no response. I tried the back door but it was locked, and so was the front, as were all the ground-floor windows. Then I spotted an open window; it was upstairs and looked like a landing window – it was too small for a bedroom, and contained clear glass, so it wasn't a toilet or bathroom. If I could reach it, I could open it wider and it was large enough for me to squeeze through. I found a ladder in one of the outbuildings and, within moments, was climbing towards my point of entry. Although the top was open, I felt it would be easier to enter through the lower half and it was the matter of a moment to raise it. The window was well maintained, I realized, and without any trouble, seconds later, I was inside. I found myself on a long landing-cum-corridor which ran the length of the rear of the house and my first act was to shout as loud as I could to announce my somewhat unusual entry.

There was no response. I stood in the corridor for a minute or so, shouting several more times as I gained my bearings, but with no response I knew it was time to begin my search. At the far end, I saw the bathroom – the door was standing open and the frosted glass window inside told me its function. I looked in. Nothing.

Along the corridor, which was carpeted with a long runner but which had no pictures or adornments on walls which hadn't been painted for decades, there were four heavy wooden doors, unpainted and all closed, while at the end opposite the bathroom, there was a staircase to the ground floor. I began to knock on each door, shouting my name and then, when I received, no response, I opened the door and peered inside. Bedroom one was more of a box room, full of surplus furnishings like chairs, chests-of-drawers and even an old grandfather clock. Bedroom two contained a chest-of-drawers, a dressing-table, a cane chair and a single bed covered with a colourful patch quilt. Hanging on the wall above the bed was a sampler dated 1812 depicting a Biblical scene and the message 'Nearer my God to Thee'. Judging by the stale smell and the closed window looking over the front of the house, it hadn't been used for years. So who had used it, if Zip never had guests?

I found him in bedroom three. He was lying in a double bed, open to the elements because he had kicked off the covers but he was wearing striped pyjamas and he was alive. His eyes followed me; he was terrified but he couldn't move...

'It's PC Rhea.' I had no idea whether my voice would mean anything to him and so I bent down, felt he was still warm and checked via his pulse that his heart was beating, if erratically. 'I'll get help.'

His mouth tried to respond but nothing came out and so I said, 'I'm going to ring for help, Mr Pentecost.' I used his formal name in these circumstances.

Using Zip's own telephone, I managed to catch Dr Williams in his surgery before he left on his rounds and he promised he'd come immediately; he suggested I call an ambulance which I did on the radio of my van after letting myself out via his kitchen door. I left it standing open for the doctor and ambulance crew, wondering if the cat would go into the house, then went back upstairs to remain with Zip. I knew better than try to move him at this point. Dr Williams would be here within minutes and so I stood near his bed, talking to him and reassuring him that help was imminent, but although he tried to speak he could not reply. I could guess what he was saying – he'd want me to get out of his house and leave him alone, he wouldn't want help and most certainly, he would have no desire to see strangers in his home. During those few minutes, I looked around the room – there was a wardrobe in the corner, a handsome walnut piece with the door closed; a chest-of-drawers was against one wall, while his familiar old clothes were hanging over a chair. His watch and a handkerchief were on the bedside cabinet and two religious samplers hung from the walls. Then I spotted a family photograph. Old and faded, it showed a young man, a young woman and a small boy.

It was a Victorian style black-and-white print, now looking distinctly brown; it had been taken in a studio, with a background looking like the garden of a stately home, and it was standing on the dressing-table beside a water jug and bowl. I thought it must be Zip and his parents. Apart from that, the room was bare with no unnecessary trimmings. No train set adorned this floor.

Then I heard a voice downstairs. 'Hello, Dr Williams here.'

'Upstairs, Doctor, through the kitchen and turn right.'

Moments later, the burly figure of Dr William Williams, in his brogues, plus fours and tweed jacket, filled the doorway and he said, 'Well, well, Zip, this is not like you, is it? So, what's the matter? Let's have a look at you.'

'I'll go downstairs,' I said, thinking that Zip and the doctor would wish for privacy.

'You've called the ambulance?' asked Williams.

'Yes, it should be here soon.'

'Good. Right, Zip, let me see if I can find out what's happened to you.'

I went downstairs and decided to feed the cat. There were some meat scraps on a plate and a pint of milk on the cold shelf in the pantry, and I found a dish in the scullery. So at least one member of the family was happy. I was debating whether to look for some hen meal when the ambulance crew arrived, two men in uniforms who'd turned up at several of my incidents.

'What is it this time, Nick?' asked Ken Sudbury, the elder of the two.

'An old man,' I said. 'He can't speak or move, he's in bed. The doctor's with him.'

'We'll wait till he comes down with instructions,' smiled Ken. 'Heart attack, is it? Stroke? He's not been attacked, has he?'

'No, nothing like that. So far as I know, he was fit and active until last night. The postman saw the curtains closed. He knew it was unusual, so he told me, and I got in through an upstairs window and found him paralysed in bed. It's more than a first-aid job, I know that!'

Heavy footsteps on the stairs announced the return of Dr Williams and he said to the ambulance crew, 'Ashfordly Hospital right away. Stroke, I think, or some form of heart attack but the fact he's alive means he's in with a chance. I'll ring ahead to announce his arrival and prepare a reception committee!'

Within five or six minutes, poor old Zip, his eyes looking both terrified and angry, was being carried on a stretcher and loaded into the ambulance which eased away smoothly as it headed for Ashfordly Cottage Hospital.

'He'll survive,' Dr Williams told me. 'His speech might be affected though, and some of his mobility. I think he's had a stroke; parts of him might be paralysed perhaps only temporarily, but whatever happens next, I think he can say goodbye to this place.'

'There's all his animals and poultry,' I said. 'And his crops...'

'Someone'll have to come in and sort things out,' the doctor said in his brusque manner. 'You'll be able to trace his relatives?'

'I don't think he has any,' I said. 'He's always lived alone, and has never let anyone in the house. I'll lock up though, and I'll tell Mr Blaketon in the post office where to find the key if anyone needs it.'

'Well, Constable, even if he does come back here, he'll be in no fit state either to look after himself or to care for his animals and plants. It'll have to go, all that lot, hens, bullocks, the cat – and the house. Look, I must be off, I've patients to visit. Call in when you can and I'll update you on the progress of Mr Pentecost.'

And with that, Dr William returned to his car and roared away to go about his daily visits. I was left with a lot of clucking hens and a cat which now seemed content, for it wandered away and lay down in a patch of sunshine near one of the sheds. I decided to feed the hens before I locked up and left. I found the hen feed in one of the outbuildings and filled the wooden troughs they used, then collected twenty-five eggs from the henhouses and decided to take them to Blaketon; I knew he bought eggs from Zip, and he could settle his account later. I fed the ducks too, and the geese, and even the pigs and bullocks, feeling happy that there were no cows to milk, and also feeling pleased I'd had a little experience of such things as a child helping on my grandfather's farm. Then I went upstairs, made sure all the lights and taps were off, closed the landing window and covered the bed Zip had used. As I was leaving the bedroom, I glimpsed the photograph I'd noticed earlier and thought it was nice that Zip had retained such an atmospheric reminder of his parents. It was such a good photo, I thought, and wondered when and where it had been taken.

I had no right to search Zip's belongings at this stage – had I been dealing with a sudden death, then I would have had to hunt through his belongings, but as he was still alive, my duties had really ended with his trip to hospital. But perhaps the date the photograph had been taken was on it? It wasn't on the front, but when I turned it over, I saw the name 'Randolph's Studio, Ashfordly' and the date, 10 October, 1919 written in white paint on the rear. Nearly fifty years ago, I thought.

Then I realized the little boy in the photograph was only about five or six years old, so if he'd been born in, say, 1913 or thereabouts, he'd now be in the region of fifty-five, give or take a year or two. But Zip was much older than that – he was at least seventy-five, or even eighty! By my reckoning, the little boy could not be Zip – so who was it? This caused me to looked closer at the faces of the trio and I saw that the man standing beside the woman was in fact a very youthful Zip! Surely that nose was the clue! That fact made sense. Zip was not the child, he was the adult! And the woman with them made this look distinctly like a family portrait. So had Zip been married and produced a son? Is that why he wanted no one in the house – was it because they might learn his secret, or had something more serious happened in the past? I recalled I had found him in a double bed, with a room nearby containing a single bed

– more evidence of a family? If Zip had had a wife, what had happened to her? And if they'd had a son, where was he? And what was the relevance of the toy train set still on the floor of that downstairs room?

I left the photo where it was but made a note of its contents in my diary and went downstairs. I found the room which contained the train set. It was like a museum with old newspapers, cuttings, photographs and toys – with the train set dominating the display. I felt rather intrusive so did not investigate further, but locked the house. After making sure it was secure and that the livestock had been given their morning feed, I left Woodford Intake and took the keys with me.

My first port of call was the post office where I acquainted Oscar Blaketon with events, and told him I would retain Zip's keys. When I mentioned my concern about the animals, however, Blaketon came to my rescue with a simple suggestion.

'Have a word with Greengrass,' he advised me. 'He and Zip are pals; they do a bit of wheeling and dealing. He'll want to know about Zip's hospitalization and you can suggest he sees to the livestock.'

'Right, I'll do that,' I assured him, then

continued with, 'Now, can I ask this? What do you know about Zip? His background in particular.'

'Very little,' he admitted. 'He comes in here once a week for his pension, and he lives alone. He earns a few bob with his enterprise, cash in hand where he can fiddle it – and that's about it. Why? Is something bothering you?'

I told him about the picture and the train set, expressing my opinions about them, but Blaketon shook his head. 'Sorry, I haven't been here long enough to know his family history, and I never came across him during the time I was at Ashfordly. You'll have to find someone in the village, someone pretty old with a good memory. Or you could try Claude? He and Zip are pals, as I said.'

'I'd better inform somebody from the chapel, too,' I added. 'He was a regular attender.'

'Have a word with Miss Trimdon at Wesley House,' he smiled. 'She's big in the chapel, and she'll pass the word around her congregation, and she'll tell Pastor Smith.'

'Thanks.' I appreciated his advice and decided to visit Claude Jeremiah Greengrass without delay. His old truck was in his yard as I motored down his bumpy drive and when he heard my arrival, he appeared from an outbuilding with Alfred at his heels and bellowed, 'It's nowt to do with me, whatever it is, and I didn't do it, so there's no need to hang about here, Constable, making the place look untidy!'

I ignored his outburst and said, 'I'm not here to quiz you, Claude, not yet! I'm here about your pal, Awd Zip.'

'Has somebody been nicking his eggs?' grinned Greengrass. 'I allus told him he should lock those hen houses at night.'

'No, he's in hospital, in a serious condition,' and as I explained to Claude, the grin vanished from his face and he became extremely concerned.

'Poor Awd Zip,' he said. 'What a thing to happen ... can I visit him?'

'I'm sure he'd like that but it would be sensible to ring up and check with the ward first.'

'Right, I'll do that. Look, it's good of you to come and tell me. Sorry I was off hand.'

'Forget it,' I said. 'Now, Claude, there are two more things.'

'Oh, no, here we go! So what am I supposed to have done now?'

'Nothing,' I laughed. 'Look, someone should see to Zip's poultry and animals, feed them and so on, collect the eggs. I wondered if you might do that for him?'

"Course I will!' he said. 'You know that. Anything to help Awd Zip. Leave it with me, Constable. The job's as good as done.'

'That's a relief.'

'So what's the other thing?' he asked cautiously.

'Has he any relatives?' I asked. 'I know he lived alone and so far as folks in the village know, he's always been alone,' and I told Claude about the photograph and train set I'd found. 'If he has a son or a wife somewhere, or some other relations, I need to find them. They should know about his illness; he's in a serious way.'

'His wife ran off with an insurance man,' said Claude. 'Years and years ago; then she got killed in a traffic accident. She was buried somewhere down south. He never even went to the funeral. You can forget her.'

'And a son? Did they have a son?'

'They did, he stayed with his dad. He was only ten when she cleared off and his dad brought him up.'

'Here in Aidensfield?'

'Oh aye, they lived where he lives now.'

'No one seems to know about this, Claude.'

'Zip never talked about it and most folks hereabouts will not know the story, they're too young. Them that did know will have forgetten about it now. But Zip fell out with the lad when he was about eighteen, summat to do with a girl, and the lad cleared off. Long before the war that was. He got married and went to live in the Lake District, got a job on the roads, and did his wartime bit with the Green Howards. But he never came back to live here; he never kept in touch with his dad, not even a Christmas card. I'd see him sometimes, if he ever came over this way, on holiday sometimes with his wife, her folks came from hereabouts. Or he'd come over when he had summat to do in connection with his work – he got a top job with the highways people and often came this way for meetings and conferences. He would sometimes call in to see me, but he never called on his dad, although he usually asked about him. And I never told Zip he'd been in Aidensfield or in this area. I kept quiet about his lad's coming and goings; I didn't want to renew old family upsets or stir things up, if you understand.'

'A sad story,' I whispered.

'Aye, it is.' Claude's face was surprisingly

sympathetic. 'I once tried to get 'em to-gether, but the lad said he would never apologize to his dad; he was at fault, he reckoned, for causing the split, and Zip never said owt about his lad to me. So there they were, daft really, but what can you do? Two stubborn beggars! Besides, Constable, it was really nowt to do with me anyroad.'

'And other relations? Are there any?'

'Nobody; Zip was an only child, and so was Zip's wife. No cousins, nowt.'

'Then we need to find this son. What was it all about then? This split?'

'The lad found himself a lass who Zip wouldn't entertain under any circum-stances. Some old family feud, I think, and she was a Catholic an' all. Two black marks against her. But the lad said he'd marry who he wanted, Catholic or not, family feud or not, and when he came up against Zip's stonewalling, he took off. He married her – and is still married to her, so far as I know, with a lovely family. Zip's missed all that, being a granddad and so on. Silly old buffer.'

'In spite of that, he must have had some feelings for his son,' I whispered. 'He had his photo by his bedside – and still has!'

'Ah, I think he regretted what he'd done,

126

specially as he got older. You say nobody ever got into his house, well, I managed to, just once. A long time ago. By accident. The door was open and I went in looking for him, but missed him 'cos he was down the hen run, but I got into his middle room and there was photos all over, of his lad. Even his wedding picture was there, cut out of the *Gazette* because he got married locally and it was pasted in a frame. A toy train set was made up on the floor ... no wonder he never wanted folks to go into the house. He played hell with me, got really angry about me wandering in and looking round and he made me promise I'd not say a word about what I'd found, and I haven't, not till now.'

'I saw that train set and photos and things. I'm sure his son does mean something to him. Thanks Claude, it helps, but he couldn't overcome his stubborn nature, could he?' I put to Claude. 'In spite of everything, he couldn't say sorry to his own flesh and blood!'

'I think he really wanted to forget the past, deep down, and renew his contacts with his son, but he didn't know where the lad was and always said it was the lad's fault and he should be the one to come forward.'

'So where is the son now? Do you know?'

'No idea,' Claude admitted. 'He never left me an address or phone number, he just turned up out of the blue from time to time. After the war, he transferred to Cheshire, I think, still on the highways, and kept getting promotion. The last I heard he was up in Northumberland. Head lad. County highways officer or some such thing, but that was a few years back.'

'He could be anywhere now.'

'He could; he moved around a lot, getting better posts. Very ambitious, he was. He's mebbe still working somewhere, he won't be at retiring age yet. And, think on, he might have in-laws hereabouts, his wife was from Maddleskirk. Shaw, she was called. Bernadette Shaw, although I never knew her family. Mebbe her folks still live there; you could check. They'll be getting on now, though. In their seventies or eighties, I'd say.'

'Now that's a starting point for me, although I'd better see if I can find him first, talk direct to him. And with that sort of high-profile job, he'd often get his picture in the papers?'

'Aye, he did, and Zip always cut 'em out whenever he saw anything – quite often the *Gazette* would do a piece about him, local lad made good type of piece and Zip would keep the cuttings.'

'Well, if he's working for a local authority somewhere, he shouldn't be hard to find, not with a name like Pentecost!' I laughed. 'I'll see what I can do. I can always ring up the Shaws in the telephone book as well, if I can't make any progress elsewhere.'

'He's a Zachariah an' all, is the lad,' beamed Claude. 'Family name, handed down to the eldest son, but he was Zachariah Aaron. Zap, as a lad. Zap and Zip...'

I thought that would make him easy to trace! I was tempted to return to Zip's house and let myself in with the key which was still in my pocket, hoping to find some evidence of his son's whereabouts, but felt it would be too intrusive at this stage. Instead, I went home to ponder how best I could set about tracing Zachariah junior. I started with a phone call to the highways department of Northumberland County Council. I was both surprised and delighted to find a man who knew Mr Pentecost, and said he'd moved on to Norfolk only two years ago. I rang the highways department at County Hall in Martineau Lane, Norwich and introduced myself.

'I'm PC Rhea from the North Riding Constabulary,' I began. 'I'm trying to trace a Mr Zachariah Pentecost.'

'We have an Alan Pentecost,' came the swift response. 'I can't say I've heard him called Zachariah!' And there was a faint chuckle in his voice.

'His middle name begins with A,' I returned swiftly, thinking fast. If I'd been christened Zachariah, I might have called myself something else. Alan sounded OK.

'Well, it must be him, he's the only Pentecost on our books.'

'It sounds like it to me. Can I talk to him please?'

'I'm sorry, he's away on holiday, and I'm not allowed to reveal his address.'

'Then can you get a message to him?'

'Yes, we could do that.'

'Good, well, my phone number is Aidensfield 277,' I began. 'Perhaps he could ring me; it is urgent.'

'I need to know the nature of the urgency, Mr Rhea, we're not in the habit of ringing our heads of departments when they're on holiday.'

'His father has had a stroke or a heart attack, and is in Ashfordly Cottage Hospital, in a bad way. I need to inform his son, he's his only relative.'

'Oh, well, in that case I can give you a contact number. That's one of the things we can allow. He's with his in-laws in a village called Maddleskirk, in the North Riding. They're called Shaw, and the phone number is Maddleskirk 305.'

'Thanks,' I breathed. 'You've been most helpful.'

'Pleased to be of help,' returned the voice. 'But are you sure his name is Zachariah?'

'The man I am seeking does have that name, yes, and so does his father, and his grandfather and his great grandfather.'

'I'm pleased my parents didn't burden me like that!' laughed my contact. 'I've the good old ordinary name of Barnabas!'

The fact that young Zachariah was in the district at this particular time was one of those extraordinary coincidences that life throws up occasionally, and instead of ringing the number, I checked the address in the telephone directory, found the Shaws lived at 17, White Horse Lane, Maddleskirk, and set off immediately. Ten minutes later, I was knocking on their front door. Mrs Shaw, a lady in her late seventies, responded and I could see the shock on her face when she found a policeman on her doorstep, surely the sign of bad news. 'I'm looking for Mr Pentecost,' I explained. 'Alan.' I decided to use the name he seemed to prefer.

'He's down the garden,' she said. 'Shall I call him, or do you want to go through?'

'I'll go through if I may,' I said, and she showed me through the house and out of the back door into a spacious garden. I could see a man working on one of the herbaceous borders, and went towards him. He was a stoutly built man, not a bit like Zip, and he had a shock of thick grey hair. He heard my approach on a gravel path and turned towards me.

'Oh-oh, trouble!' He smiled at the sight of the uniform. 'Has the office burnt down or something? Or has one of my bridges or roundabouts been demolished by a lorry?'

'Nothing like that,' I responded; then after introducing myself, I said, 'It's a family matter, but before I start, is your full name Zachariah Aaron Pentecost?'

'You have done your homework, Constable! It is, but I prefer Alan!'

'I'm not sure how to begin this,' I said, then I took Zip's house keys out of my pocket and held them up before Alan. 'These are the keys to your father's house.' His face became serious and he knew I bore bad news.

'My father?'

'Zachariah Isaac Pentecost of Woodford Intake. Zip, as he's known to everyone. He's had a seizure of some kind, heart attack, stroke, or something along those lines. He's in Ashfordly Cottage Hospital. He is your father, isn't he?'

'In name only. He threw me out years ago, Mr Rhea; we've had no contact since. He doesn't want anything to do with me, and never has had for years.'

'You're his only relative, Mr Pentecost. And if I told you there is something inside his house which would make you want to see him, would you do that? Go in and have a look before you do anything else, then decide whether you want to visit him in hospital. One of you has to make the break-through, mend fences, or whatever they call it. Now's your chance. And fate has put you almost on the doorstep at this very moment, hasn't it? Isn't that an omen of some sort?'

I held the keys in the palm of my hand which I extended before him, willing him to accept them.

'What about the livestock?' he said. 'His hens and things.'

'Claude Jeremiah Greengrass has promised to look after them,' I assured him.

'I drive past his house every time I come to this part of the world, and I've often wanted to call in and talk to him, but I've never had the courage, Mr Rhea ... he said he never wanted to see me again, I was only eighteen ... he meant it, you know.'

'I think he might have regretted it ever since, so now's your chance to find out,' I smiled. 'He's in Ashfordly Cottage Hospital; you'll have to ring to see how he's progressing, and for visiting times.'

He expelled a huge sigh, a sigh of relief I felt, which was also a means of smothering a bout of emotion which was even now welling up inside him. He took the keys and said, 'It's been nearly forty years, Mr Rhea, he's a great-granddad now. I'll ring the hospital but first I'll go to the house,' and I could see moisture in his eyes. 'I've often wondered what happened to my train set.'

Chapter 5

When Arnold Merryweather broke his leg one autumn, it meant he had to recruit a team of reserve drivers to ensure he could fulfil the programme of services advertised by his bus company. There was his market-day run on Fridays for example, during which he collected passengers from the surrounding villages and transported them, and sometimes their wares, to Ashfordly market. His bus, invariably full, arrived at 10.30 a.m. and departed at 3.30 p.m., thus allowing the passengers time to do their shopping and banking, visit the hairdresser, dentist or accountant and have lunch. His popular York-and-back service ran on Wednesdays with a similar timetable, and on special occasions he would send coaches to the races at Thirsk, Redcar, York or Beverley. In addition, he arranged trips to Blackpool illuminations, the autumn colours of the Lake District and the walks within Castle Howard; there were seaside events and entertainments at Scarborough and

Bridlington, shopping trips to Harrogate, Leeds or Newcastle, and on one occasion he even took an outing to London for a visit to the Tower, Westminster Abbey, Oxford Street and other traditional sights, venues and shops in the capital. There is a story of Arnold standing in the crowd on the pavement in Regent Street as he was trying in vain to cross the busy road. Nearby was a policeman who recognized the flat-capped Arnold as a 'country chap from up north' and, in an attempt to be friendly, gazed across the road and said, 'It's very busy, isn't it?'

'Aye,' said Arnold. 'I'm not surprised, there's a bus trip in from Aidensfield, you know.'

During Arnold's incapacity, however, he had little trouble finding stand-in drivers. Apart from being paid for their work, it meant such volunteers secured a free trip to interesting places so Arnold generally had no shortage of volunteers. Then it transpired he wanted a driver for a regular mystery tour scheduled for a Saturday during that September. This was one of his more popular events – Arnold himself invariably acted as driver on this occasion and took his bus over the Pennines into the

Lake District so that his passengers could enjoy the rich autumn colours of the spectacular scenery in the September sunshine. Although the outing was always scheduled as a mystery tour, most of the passengers were regulars who knew that Arnold would head for the Lakes on that particular Saturday, although, should the weather be foggy or heavy with rain, it was understood that he might divert to some other unknown destination.

On this occasion, he found that all his small pool of reliable reserve drivers had previous commitments; his own leg, still in plaster, meant he could not drive and so, unable to guarantee a driver, he became very concerned that he might let down his regular mystery tourers, most of whom were ladies of a certain age who had grey hair and were blessed with husbands who 'reckoned nowt' to bus trips. Many were members of the WI, for example, and others were relations of those WI members.

The trip had been fully booked for several weeks. All fifty-two seats had been taken and indeed there was a waiting list of eager ladies. Part of the attraction, I was to learn later, was that Arnold had installed a television set in his coach so his passengers

137

could relax and be entertained on their long homebound journeys.

For a bus – or indeed any other motor vehicle – to contain a television set was a fairly new idea and was quite within the law as laid down in Section 108 of the Construction and Use Regulations, 1963 and 1964, although the device had to be fitted so the driver could not see the screen, and it had to be presented in such a way that no other driver was distracted by it.

In his quest to find a suitable driver, therefore, Arnold decided to visit the pub to ask if George knew anyone who might wish to earn a few pounds – an ex-bus driver or retired policeman, perhaps? There must be someone who'd welcome a chance to drive one of the most up-to-date buses in this part of Yorkshire. After all, in Arnold's expert opinion, a bus equipped with television was the height of luxury. It was perhaps unfortunate that as Arnold stomped his way to the bar counter at eleven one morning, Claude Jeremiah Greengrass was also entering the pub with his dog Alfred in tow. George observed them both and graciously smiled a welcome.

'Morning, gents,' he beamed, wondering if there was going to be a race *not* to be first to reach the bar. Greengrass would probably opt to arrive just too late to buy the first round – but he didn't. Most unusually, he was first at the bar.

'Morning, George,' nodded Arnold, as he plodded towards the place where money had to be exchanged.

'By gum, Arnold,' – Greengrass momentarily ignored George and directed all his attention towards Arnold, perhaps sensing that all was not well within the world of Arnold Merryweather Coaches Ltd – 'this is a rare occasion, you coming into the pub so early on a morning. What can I get you?'

The fact the Greengrass had ordered the drinks suggested he had spotted a business opportunity in connection with Arnold's abnormal leg.

'Well, I haven't really come for a drink, it's a bit early for me ... I never drink during the day.'

'That's your rule for when you're driving, Arnold,' beamed Greengrass. 'But now you've been grounded with that leg of yours, you can surely indulge in a quick half or summat.'

'Well, if you insist.'

'I do, for an old mate. Two pints, George, if you please,' beamed Greengrass, ignoring

Arnold's reference to a half. The fact that he ordered pints was a further indication that he had recognized a chance to earn a few pounds – he'd probably heard that Arnold was seeking relief drivers. As George organized the drinks, Claude turned to Arnold who had now reached at the bar counter and hoisted himself on to a high stool. Claude joined him.

'So if you've not come for a drink, Arnold, what have you come for? Or is it summat too secret for me to know about?'

'No, there's nothing secret about it, Claude. I'm short of a qualified driver and wondered if George might know somebody who'd step in at short notice. It's that autumn mystery tour of mine, you know the one, it's when I go to the Lake District and visit all the lakes. It's on Saturday and I haven't found anybody yet; everybody seems committed.'

'A driver? Well, you need look no further!' and Claude puffed out his chest. 'I can make myself available on Saturday and there's nowt I like better than a good mystery tour, especially in the Lake District.'

'Well, I don't really want to bother somebody like you, a man who's very busy anyway…'

140

The truth was that Arnold knew of some of Claude's previous bus-driving excursions and he wasn't all that keen to risk an outing with Greengrass at the wheel. There was the time he'd got lost on one mystery tour, and another occasion when he took a party of pensioners to the races when they should have gone to the official opening of a shopping centre. Understandably, Arnold was somewhat wary, but a gentle bribe, in the shape of a pint glass, was on its way from Greengrass. Claude accepted the pints from George and passed one of them to Arnold.

'I just wanted a half, Claude.'

'I don't buy halves, Arnold,' he said witheringly. 'It's against my religion. Look, let's be straight about all this. We've been mates for years. If I can't step in at short notice when you're stuck for help, then who can? Just you tell me that!'

'I'm sure I could find a good driver who'd love an excuse for a trip to the Lakes,' interrupted George, recognizing Arnold's reluctance to rely on Claude. 'There's no need to impose on Claude...'

'Impose on me? Who's imposing on me?' blustered Claude. 'I'm volunteering my services for an old mate. Say no more, Arnold. The job's as good as done. So where do I pick up the bus?'

It was at this point that I entered the pub – on duty. George later told me about the conversation which had preceded my arrival. I was touring all the licensed premises on my patch to alert licensees to the theft of a load of whisky from a delivery truck. It had been parked overnight in Scarborough and someone had unloaded it completely without anyone noticing the heist. It was possible the thieves might try to dispose of bottles of cut-price whisky to landlords and off-licences in the locality; if anyone offered the stolen bottles on my patch, I hoped I would be informed.

'Going somewhere, Claude?' I asked, as I heard him refer to picking up a bus.

'Not that it's owt to do with you, Constable, this is a private matter, but Arnold here's in need of a good mate to get him out of a hole, and I've just volunteered.'

'So how is the leg, Arnold?' I asked. He had managed to hoist himself on to the bar stool with his leg sticking out and resting on the rungs of the one next to it.

'I'll be getting this plaster off next week, so it shouldn't be long before I'm back at work, but I need a driver for this Saturday–'

'And I've said I'll do it for an old mate,'

beamed Claude.

'Arnold was wondering if I knew any good drivers who might fancy a run, it would have to be somebody with a PSV driver's licence,' George said pointedly.

'I've got one,' Claude interrupted. 'And an HGV licence, and I'm licensed for motor bikes, road rollers, mowing machines and track-laying vehicles.'

'So you can drive anything, Claude?' smirked George.

'I can, so a modern, well-equipped bus like yours will be a doddle, Arnold. Especially one with a television set, there'll be no need for a sing-song or owt like that to keep 'em entertained.'

At this stage, Claude emptied his glass and plonked it on the counter with a loud bang; Arnold took the hint and said, 'My round, George, but I won't have another, one's enough for me at this time of day. How about you, Constable?'

'No thanks, I'm on duty,' I said.

And so poor old Arnold found himself inveigled into accepting Claude's offer; Claude said he would call round at Arnold's depot later in the week to be given a full briefing about the trip. I acquainted them with news of the whisky raid and all

143

promised they'd keep their ears and eyes open, promising to inform me if any crime-busting information came their way. Arnold left the pub to return to his office, I left to visit the Hopbind at Elsinby with news of the whisky raid, while Claude remained to have another pint or perhaps two aided by a pork pie and a pickled onion while dreaming about guiding a television-equipped luxury coach through Lakeland's spectacular mountain scenery on one of Arnold's tours.

I felt a little sorry for Arnold, having Claude thrust upon him in this manner, but accepted that Arnold, being a businessman, should have been a little tougher in rejecting Claude's offer. But the deed was done and I could not see what problems Claude might create, apart from getting lost *en route*. That would be a temporary blip, however, for eventually he'd find his way home, perhaps with a few unscheduled stops. Whatever happened, I reasoned, it was unlikely to be serious. On the Saturday morning in question, I was on duty and happened to arrive at the village hall as Claude was gathering his customers in the car-park and checking them as they boarded the coach. Arnold was there too, issuing tickets, marking off names and collecting fares.

'Morning all,' I shouted, above the excited noise of lots of chattering ladies.

I could not see any men among them – doubtless the notion of joining an outing of the WI, albeit disguised as a mystery tour, had not appealed to the menfolk of the locality. Perhaps they had other matters to interest them?

'Morning, Constable,' greeted Arnold. 'A nice day, ideal for a mystery tour.'

'Perfect,' I responded, adding, 'So don't get lost, Claude!'

'Would I?' he retorted. 'Anybody would think I don't know my way around this country...'

I left them to their boarding as I popped into the village hall for a chat with the secretary about allowing bingo and tombola on a forthcoming event. I was on day duties today which meant I finished at five. That was a most welcome change because normally, I'd be working till midnight or 1 a.m. on a Saturday, but today there were no dances on my patch. An early finish would be welcome – Mary had booked Mrs Quarry, our regular baby-sitter, which meant we could go out for a drink and a bar snack this evening.

As the village hall secretary and I discussed the legal situation about bingo and tombola, I saw Arnold's busful of ladies leave the car-park with Claude at the wheel and Alfred standing on his hind legs to peer out of the windscreen. Arnold returned to his office and shortly afterwards, I went home for lunch. My afternoon patrol would encompass some of the more outlying villages and I still had a few pubs to visit on my mission to find any trace of the stolen whisky. It promised to be a quiet Saturday unless there was a plane crash on the moors, or a fire in Ashfordly Hospital, or traffic accident somewhere, or a sudden death, or a cat stuck up a tree...

Over lunch, though, Mary asked, 'Where will you be going this afternoon, Nick?'

'A bit of a round tour really, quite gentle, and chiefly confined to the outskirts of my beat,' I said. 'Whemmelby, Shelvingby, Craydale, Ploatby ... and I have some paper-work to drop into the office at Ashfordly while I'm out and I might find time to call at Brantsford. Why? Do you want something?'

'It's not important,' she told me. 'But if you're anywhere near a bookmaker's, I wonder if you could put a pound each way on a horse for me?'

'You? Betting?' I smiled, somewhat puzzled.

'It's the St Leger this afternoon, at Doncaster,' she reminded me. 'I saw it in the paper. There's a horse called Mary's Joy running. With a name like that, I thought I might invest a couple of pounds on it.'

'It's one of those daft bets that might just work!' I laughed. 'All right, I'll see what I can do, but I mustn't go into a betting shop to place a bet while I'm in uniform. I'll see if Alf Ventress can help, he's bound to know someone who can put it on for you.'

Now I realized why there were no men on that bus outing. They'd all want to stay at home to watch the racing on television, or even drive to Doncaster for the event. They might even have gone to the races on another bus trip with a rival company. After lunch, and with Mary's request in mind, I decided to visit Ashfordly Police Office before heading for the hills and moors; I had some reports to deliver and would use the opportunity give Mary's money to Alf in the hope he could place the bet. That done, I could head for Craydale and elsewhere on my whisky theft tour.

When I called at Ashfordly Police Office,

Alf said he could help through a friend of his and so I gave him Mary's two pounds for an each-way bet on Mary's Joy, then set about my tour of the outskirts of my beat. I had no idea of the result of the St Leger and, not being a betting man, I had forgotten all about the race until I returned home. Mary was jumping up and down with excitement when I went into the house, and she said, 'Did you get my bet on, Nick?'

'Yes, Alf said he'd see to it,' I assured her.

'Oh, lovely, lovely.' She beamed with happiness.

'You sound very pleased...' and then it dawned on me that she must have heard the result. 'Did it win? I haven't heard the results.'

'Yes, by a long way,' she said. 'It was on the radio ... odds of twenty-five to one, they said, an outsider. That means I'll have won quite a lot.'

'Crikey! Yes, well over twenty-five pounds ... and you get something extra because you backed it each way. I don't know how much extra, I'm not a betting man, but whatever happens, you're in the money, Mary!'

'I'll treat us tonight, Nick, and there'll be enough for something for the children.'

'You should get yourself something,' I told

her. 'You don't get many treats, so don't go spending it all on me or the family. Get yourself a nice new outfit or a dress or a hairdo or something.'

Without any prompting from me, Alf had collected Mary's winnings and around seven that evening, the duty constable, fortunately patrolling the district in the GP car, arrived at our house with a plain brown envelope containing Mary's winnings – more than thirty pounds – and a little note from Alf saying he'd backed Mary's Joy too; he'd won a like amount. And so, in a mood for celebrating, we left Mrs Quarry in charge of the children and walked to the pub for the evening. Even though it meant drinking and socializing on my own patch, something I tried to avoid, it meant I did not have to worry about driving home after a beer or two.

The bar was full of regulars and among them I spotted Arnold Merryweather with a few of his friends, playing dominoes. We had a lovely relaxed meal followed by Black Forest gateau and coffee and were settling down to a liqueur as a modest means of completing our celebrations when the door burst open and in stumbled Claude Jeremiah Greengrass as if all the hounds in hell were chasing him. Indeed, Alfred was chasing him, but quietly.

'I need a double whisky, George, and quick about it!' he blurted, but even as he reached the counter, the door burst open and a procession of angry women followed him, waving umbrellas, calling him names and demanding their rightful dues.

'What's all this, then?' asked George, with more than a hint of amusement.

'All what?' Claude feigned innocence, but a ferocious-looking woman with a large hat and an ugly umbrella, was hard behind him and she began to beat Claude about the shoulders with her brolly. She was Mrs Leatherwell, widow of a former blacksmith, and a lady once noted for her own ability to shoe a reluctant cart horse.

'You know what!' she bellowed, where-upon she had the immediate attention of everyone present and thrashed Claude again. 'Our money, Claude. You promised ... we're not going home until we get it, are we, girls? And it's no good running away like this, sheltering in the pub, we saw you come in ... pretending you were coming back with the cash ... you can't trick us that easily, Claude.'

'I'd forgotten I've none in the house, so I

thought I might borrow some from a pal or two in here, you know, good old friends of long standing...'

'Well, we're waiting,' she said, laying the brolly on the counter and folding her arms while making sure she stood close enough to Claude to deal with him in the event of any deviation from his promises.

'George?' Claude's voice had a distinctive tone of pleading to it. 'Any chance of a loan, a small one, just over the weekend. Till I get to the bank?'

'No chance,' George made his decision immediately.

A deathly hush then descended upon the bar as everyone heard this exchange and awaited Claude's next move. He blinked and blushed and twisted and turned and squirmed and sighed, then Mrs Leatherwell, taking advantage of the lull in conversation, said, 'Claude owes money to us all, every one of us.'

'How much?' asked George.

'A hundred and thirty pounds between us,' snapped Mrs Leatherwell.

'A hundred and thirty?' cried George. 'After a bus trip? How on earth did you get into this mess, Claude?'

'Well, I said we could have a sweepstake

on the result of the St Leger, and because we had a television in the bus we could watch the race. I mean, it was going to be easy – put all the runners' names in a hat, put the punters' names in another hat and make sure they've all got a horse. Some might have the same horse, but that doesn't matter ... half a crown a time with a first, second and third prize. Five pound first prize, two pound ten for second and twenty-five bob for third.'

'Neat idea,' said George, who added, 'And that would leave a nice little profit of four pounds ten for you?'

'Ah, well, a feller needs to have a bit for thinking of it, expenses, you know.'

'So what went wrong, Claude?' George persisted.

'Well, they didn't want a sweepstake, they said it produced only one winner as a rule, they wanted to bet, like they do on race tracks. So I said I'd run a book, not with big money like they do on the track, but just summat to entertain the ladies on the trip...'

'Making up your own odds?'

'Yes, well, it was the only way, George. I mean, in the big race there was runners at fifty to one, and some at thirty to one and so on, so I took all those below the bar and made my own odds. The biggest was ten to one – and I made it a five bob stake for all, straight win.'

'So a lady placing five bob on the horse of her choice would win two pounds ten?' smiled George. 'And if everyone on the bus took part, you'd make a handsome profit of thirteen pounds?'

'Right. A feller has to earn his living somehow.'

'And the chances of all of them picking the same winner are very remote, I'd say?'

'You would think so, wouldn't you?' he sighed.

Mrs Leatherwell took up the story. 'Well, George, we thought it was a wonderful idea. Claude had a list of runners out of the paper and we all made a choice and paid him five shillings, then we pulled into a lay-by to watch the race.'

'The trouble was they all bet on the same horse,' Claude groaned. 'Would you believe it ... all because Mary Ruddock stood up and said her daughter had produced a baby girl ... so she was going to bet on Mary's Joy which I'd got at ten to one.'

'So we all bet on Mary's Joy,' beamed Mrs Leatherwell. 'And that means we've all won two pounds ten each – which is what we're waiting for Claude to pay us.'

'It comes to a hundred and thirty quid!' sighed Claude. 'And I only took thirteen in bets...'

'Claude,' said a man's voice in the bar, 'you won't have heard, but you won the Ashfordly Conservative Club's sweepstake on the St Leger. You drew Mary's Joy. You've won fifty pounds. I've got your winnings here.'

And the fellow walked forward with a fistful of money, but as he was about to hand it to Claude, Mrs Leatherwell snatched it.

'Fifty down.' She glared at Claude. 'And the thirteen you took on bets. That's sixty-three for us. Just another sixty-seven to keep us happy!'

'There's the tips we collected on the bus,' chipped in one lady. 'A shilling each. That's another two pounds twelve shillings,' and she passed over a little bag of coins.

'Just another sixty-four pounds eight shillings to go,' said Mrs Leatherwell.

'There's your wages, Claude, for the trip.' Arnold managed to stand up in spite of his pot leg. 'Five pounds ten as I promised. Here,' and Mrs Leatherwell rushed forward to seize that money.

'That leaves fifty-eight pounds eighteen

shillings,' Mrs Leatherwell was now enjoying this and, as I wondered how Claude was going to raise that amount, another man, a timber merchant said, 'Claude, I owe you for six loads of logs, a fiver each if you remember. Birch and hawthorn. That's another thirty.' And he came forward and handed the money straight to Mrs Leatherwell. 'Twenty-eight pounds eighteen shillings to go, Claude.'

Bernie Scripps now stood up and said, 'Claude, you did those five driving jobs for me last month, I've not made up my accounts but if I pay you now, it'll help Mrs Leatherwell and her ladies, won't it?'

'Aye it might, but it won't help me next month when I've got my bills to pay and when I'd be expecting money from you...'

But his plea was in vain. Bernie handed a further fifteen pounds to her and she beamed, 'I'm really enjoying this and won't our ladies be pleased. So that's another fifteen pounds, Claude. Thirteen pounds eighteen shillings to go!'

George now entered the fray. 'Seeing we're all helping Claude like this, I owe you for eggs, Claude, a month's supply. Twelve pounds fifteen shillings, by my reckoning. Here,' and he opened the till, made a note of the amount he was extracting and handed the money to Mrs Leatherwell.

'Thank you, George.' she oozed. 'Now, Claude, we're on the home straight. 'One pound three shillings to go. Twenty-three bob, Claude, and we're all square. And I'm not leaving here till I get it.'

There was complete silence in the bar as we all observed this scenario being played out before our eyes, but now everyone was watching Claude. He cast around in the hope that someone else might produce a life-saving donation of some sort, but eventually, when no one volunteered, he dug into a small inside pocket of his coat. He ferretted around for what seemed an eternity and eventually hauled out a crumpled pound note wrapped around a half-crown. Without a word, he passed it to Mrs Leatherwell.

'Sixpence to go, Claude.' She stood her ground, immovable and unflinching as she held out her hand. Claude then began to search all his other pockets, dragging out a filthy handkerchief, toothless comb, keys, bits of string, old screws and nuts, several toffees, a pocket knife and finally a three-penny bit along with three pennies. Without a word, he passed them over to her.

'That's it!' she beamed. 'Right ladies, we've got our money. Come along, we can't be seen hanging around in the pub, it's time to go home.'

And off they went. Suddenly, a ripple of applause sounded as they filed from the pub, and Claude tried to shrug off the episode, saying, 'Well, there we are. Greengrass always pays his dues. Thanks everybody ... it's a relief, I'll tell you, to know I'm paid up to date!'

'You're not,' snapped George. 'There's that whisky you ordered when you came in, and if my memory serves me right, you owe for a couple of pints for yesterday lunchtime and then there's a pork pie...'

'I need a drink!' sighed Claude.

'Allow me,' said Arnold Merryweather. 'Claude, you've given my ladies a day's outing they'll remember all their lives and on top of that, they've come home with a profit in their handbags. It wouldn't surprise me next year if they specially ask for you to be their driver.'

'Don't even think about it!' growled Claude.

One of the most frequent matters in the daily routine of a 1960s police officer was dealing with reports of lost and found property. If someone discovered an object in a public place, there was always a chance it had been stolen and thrown away, or even hidden to be collected later. The police would search their records to check whether the found property had been the subject of theft; indeed, police records are rich with stories of children or dog-walkers finding stolen silverware, jewellery or other valuables concealed behind hedgerows or even in rabbit holes, often awaiting collection by the thieves. In those cases, the police would hide nearby and wait for the thieves and, in this way, they caught a high proportion.

The police were often involved if someone's property went missing; it might have been stolen, or it might have merely been lost or mislaid, so it was fairly common for a loser to notify the police. Quite often, it was difficult to ascertain whether someone had merely lost an item or whether it had been stolen – purses lost from pockets or shopping baskets, for example, might have been skilfully removed by a pickpocket – or they may merely have been lost. It was always necessary for the police to make a distinction between lost property and stolen property – if an article had been stolen, it meant a crime had been committed and the recording of this was important from a statistical point of view, as was its eventual detection. I am sure that many stolen items were recorded merely as lost, due simply to a lack of evidence which might support an allegation of theft.

When Claude Jeremiah Greengrass came stomping into Ashfordly Police Station at noon to report a theft, therefore, I had to decide whether or not he had merely mislaid the article in question, or whether indeed it had been stolen. I was performing a four-hour tour of duty in Ashfordly that Monday morning.

'So this is where you're hiding!' he blustered as he ambled towards the counter and realized I was standing behind it. 'I've been to your house; I've searched all over Aidensfield and so I've had to come all the way here, looking for a constable. You blokes are never there when you're wanted, and you're allus there when you're not wanted.'

'Is there something you want, Claude?'

'I've had a theft, that's what, and I want summat done about it.'

'Well, I'll do what I can. So what have you lost?'

'I haven't lost it, I've had it stolen.'

159

'You're reporting a crime then?'

'I am,' he said with determination. 'And I can't get in my house until you blokes catch the thief and get it back.'

'Catching thieves is often easier said than done.' I reached for a pad of notepaper to take details before transferring the information to the official form known as a Crime Report. 'Now, full name and address. I know that. So what have you had stolen, Claude?'

'My door key. The key to my back door. The only key to my back door.'

'Your key? Stolen? You didn't leave it in the door, did you?'

'Would I be so daft? No, I did not leave it in the door. I locked the door and because young David Stockdale is helping me today, I said I'd leave it handy for him to collect so he could let himself in and get summat to eat, or attend to the needs of nature or whatever. Anyroad, it's gone.'

'You mean *he* says it's gone?'

'No, I mean *I* say it's gone! This is getting to be hard work. Look, I've only the one key for that door so if I'm away and David wants to be in while he's helping out, I leave it handy. He knows where to find it, and he puts it back there when he's finished, so I

160

can let myself in when I get home.'

'So you put the key in a safe hiding place, where David would find it, and when he got there, the key was missing?'

'By gum, you're sharp this morning, Constable. Yes, that's it.'

'Presumably David came to tell you, which is why you are here?'

'Yes. I was working in Briggsby plantation, earning a bit of extra by helping to fell timber for Ashfordly Estate and he found me, then said he couldn't get in for his ten o'clocks so could I let him have the key. I told him where I'd left it; he said he'd looked and it wasn't there, so somebody must have pinched it. I quizzed him but thought I'd better go back and check for myself. You can't rely on David, not really. But the lad was right, it was missing. It couldn't leave on its own accord so somebody must have pinched it. I had to give him the day off – he's been eating prunes and has to be near a loo all day, so I've come here to report a robbery.'

'Hardly a robbery, Claude,' I said. 'Robberies are when somebody threatens you, or uses force to steal from you – so where did you hide the key?'

'Look, is this likely to take much longer?

It's costing me money, all this time away from work. I thought you'd blokes would all leap into your cars and jump on to your motor bikes and go out looking for my key, set up road blocks or summat and mebbe even catch the bloke who's nicked it before he gets too far away.'

'All in good time, Claude, I need lots of details first. So where did you hide it?'

'In the guttering.'

'Guttering? What guttering?'

'At the back of the house, on that scullery roof. Above that little back window ... it's low enough for David to reach into without getting a ladder. I allus put it there for him, and it's never gone missing before.'

'And what time was this? When you put it there?'

'Time? Why do you want to know that?' he spluttered.

'It's for my Crime Report,' I said. 'If it has been stolen, we need to know the relevant time, just in case we catch the villain and he comes up with an alibi.'

'Half seven this morning,' he said.

'And what time was it known to be missing?'

'When David wanted to get into the house.'

162

'And what time was that?'

'How should I know? I wasn't there.'

'What time did you check?'

'Elevenish.'

'That'll do for me,' I said. 'I need your evidence that it was missing, and not just misplaced. Now, Claude, what kind of key is it?'

'Kind of key? It's a door key, I've told you that. Back-door key if you want it chapter and verse. I never use my front door, it's allus locked, and I doubt if I could find a key for it. And so far as I know, this key doesn't work on both doors. But to be honest, I've never tried it ... mebbe I should, eh? When you blokes find it.'

'I mean, is it a Yale key? Or a key for a mortise lock? Or some other kind of key? Is it made of brass or bronze or cast iron, or is it chromium-plated? Is there any kind of identifying mark on it? Manufacturer's name perhaps, or some other mark, or even a dab of paint or a scratch. If I, or any of my colleagues, come across your key, we need to know where it's come from and we need to prove it's yours.'

'I had no idea you'd make this kind of fuss, Constable. Look, it's just an ordinary key, there's nowt special about it.'

'Except you can't get into your house without it,' I smiled.

'That does make it special in some way, or important.'

I gave him a piece of scrap paper and a pencil, and asked him to try and draw some kind of image, hopefully about the actual size of the missing key. He produced a fairly accurate reproduction from which I saw it was a mortise key with a shank about four inches long, with an open oval design at the terminal end and a reasonably intricate three-pronged device for the tenon. It was probably made from iron but most of it was very shiny through constant use.

'I don't know exactly how old it is,' he said. 'But the house was built in 1762 and it wouldn't surprise me if that door's the same age and, as I've never replaced the lock, I reckon it goes back a bit.'

'Right.' After writing down these details, I asked, 'And what is its value?'

'Value? How do I know? It's invaluable to me, I'll tell you that much.'

'I need a monetary value for my report,' I said. 'What would it cost to get it replaced?'

'Search me! I've never had to replace it before.'

'Let's say ten shillings,' I said. 'Right, I

think that's all I need, Claude. I'll file this in our records and details will be circulated to all our officers. But if you do find it, you will let us know, won't you?'

'Find it? I thought it was your job to find it! Do you mean to tell me you're not going out to look for it? Search suspects' homes, interview likely villains, make enquiries, turn over the whole of Aidensfield, that sort of thing?'

'When I've finished my tour of duty here in Ashfordly, I'll go back to Aidensfield and commence enquiries,' I assured him. 'I'll want to talk to David to see if he noticed anyone around the house, and I want to chat to others who might have passed your house since you hid the key this morning – milk-lorry driver, postman, early morning workers coming through the village and so on. And I need to make a thorough search of the scene of the crime.'

'Search? I've already searched! Me and David.'

'It might have fallen down a drain pipe or got hidden under a leaf or in the debris in the guttering.'

'So what do I do in the meantime?'

'It might be an idea if you got a new lock,' I suggested. 'Although, to be honest, if a thief has made off with your key, he might already have used it to gain entry and steal things.'

'But I won't know, will I? If he's got inside and rifled through my treasures and antiques, I'll not know until I can get into the house, and I can't get into the house until you blokes have found my key! I'm not having much success, am I? With you lot ... while you're sitting on your backside asking daft questions, thieves could be disposing of my personal belongings even as we speak.'

'I shall be finished in Ashfordly in about half an hour,' I said. 'And I'll get cracking on the case the minute I return to Aidensfield. And, as I said, if you do find the key yourself, or if David comes across it, please let us know.'

'I don't know why I bother with the constabulary,' he muttered, as he turned on his heel and left. 'I'd have been better conducting my own enquiries – and I have searched the scene of the crime, as you put it. Me and David, not just one either. It's not there, I can tell you that. That's why I came here, to get some kind of service as us rate-payers are entitled to. I know the key's not there, that's why I'm here.'

'How will you get into the house if we

don't find it?' I called after him.

'A sledgehammer seems a good idea right now!' he muttered, as he vanished, banging the door behind himself.

Before I finished my stint in the office, Sergeant Craddock returned from a trip to Eltering where he'd been to a half-day crime prevention conference with other sub-divisional and sectional officers, and when he saw my notes about Claude's key, he said, 'I don't think we can record this as a crime, PC Rhea, there's no evidence that the key has been stolen. Knowing Greengrass and David, they'll have managed to lose it somewhere. I'll bet it's in one of their pockets, or they'll have put it down somewhere and forgotten where. Classify it as a lost key, PC Rhea, nothing else. I think an entry in the lost property register should suffice.'

Following those instructions, I made an entry in the lost property register and, for the time being, did not formally record the event as a crime. I wanted to visit Claude's house at Hagg Bottom and see for myself the scene of the alleged crime and went there immediately I left Ashfordly. When I got to the house, both Claude and David were present, each circling the building with their backs bent as they scoured the ground for any sign of the missing key. Claude saw me and his eyes brightened, but I had to disappoint him by saying, 'Sorry, Claude, I haven't come with good news. I want you to show me the scene of the crime.'

'Anybody would think I'd been burgled or robbed, or murdered or summat the way you describe it as the scene of the crime. It's guttering on my scullery, nowt else, there's no blood or weapons or clues, nowt like that.'

He led me to the rear of the house.

Like all moorland houses, the rear roof, invariably facing north, sloped much closer to the ground than the roof at the front; this was a form of protection against the severe winter weather, and beneath that roof were small rooms like the scullery, kitchen, pantry and various store-rooms, including lavatories in some of the modernized houses. The guttering was about six feet from the ground and he led me to a point above the scullery window.

'I put it in there.' He pointed to the place. 'David knew it would be there – but it wasn't.'

'Have you looked into the guttering?' I asked, for it was just too high for any of us to peer into, although within easy reach of a hand search.

'Looked? No, I felt with my fingers, like I allus do, and David allus does.'

'Show me.' And he obliged, dipping his fingers into the guttering, the base of which was dry, and then moving his hand along in both directions, producing only a few silver birch leaves and a fir cone. I decided I needed to look and after asking him for a ladder, he produced one and I climbed it to peer into the guttering. He was right. There was no sign of the key, and the downfall pipe was some ten feet away. This discharged its water on to a grassy patch where there was no drain and I searched it, but there was no key.

'Satisfied?' he almost smirked. 'I do know what I'm talking about, you know. If I say my key's been nicked, then been nicked it has been.'

'The thing that puzzles me, Claude, is why anyone would steal your key from here? Who would know where to find it? And has the house been ransacked?'

'No it hasn't, and no thanks to you. I've looked through the windows nothing looks disturbed. All the doors and windows are shut. But my key's gone, stolen...'

'I hope you're going to fit new locks,' I

reminded him.

'I am, I got one from Ashfordly on my way home but I thought if I could find my key, I wouldn't have to break in and could still fit new locks. This new un's got a spare key so David can have his own and it'll save all this hassle.'

'The sooner you get it fitted the better,' I said. 'But what I can't work out is why anyone would steal your key while you're out, and not use it? I mean, if a thief took it, he'd want to make use of it at the first opportunity, not wait until the householder returned. In my mind, Claude, it doesn't add up.'

'I don't care whether you can add up or not, my key's gone, I haven't got it and neither has David. That hiding place is the only spot it could be and it isn't, which, in my book, means somebody's found it and cleared off with it. But now I'm going to get in through a bedroom window which happens to have a loose catch.'

I waited as he took the ladder to one of the front bedroom windows and it was the work of a moment to insert the blade of his pocket knife between the two halves, flick open the catch and raise the bottom half high enough for him to clamber through.

Moments later, I heard him rattling the back door and then he shouted, 'I've got a crowbar in here, I'll force the socket off the doorpost...'

There were sounds of groaning and shouting, of iron against wood and iron against iron, and then a splintering sound as the hasp of the ancient lock was forced out of the old wood. And with that, the door swung open, the lock still in position with its tongue protruding, but nothing into which to put that tongue. I asked David if he'd seen anyone hanging about the place either today or on previous occasions, and he said he'd never noticed anything suspicious, nor had he seen strangers or ramblers wandering around the rear of the building. After thanking David, I told Claude, 'I'll commence enquiries in the village, Claude.'

'About time too!' he grunted.

I left them to their task of fitting the new lock and repairing the door post, then returned home for a late lunch. That afternoon I pottered about Aidensfield on foot, asking residents if any suspicious strangers had been seen in the locality, but drew a blank. At four-thirty, with my shift complete, I returned home. I rang Ashfordly Police Station to book off duty formerly, adding that I had not solved the mystery of the great Greengrass felony. I expressed a view that there was something very odd about this lost property – for a key to vanish from such a place seemed highly unlikely, particularly as it had not been used to effect entry. I tended to agree with Sergeant Craddock that a crime did not seem likely but equally, it seemed strange that the key could have been 'lost' from such a location. I had a feeling that either Claude or David had mislaid it, and had forgotten they had done so. I felt confident it would reappear in the not-too-far distant future.

In fact, it turned up later that evening. I had just finished my evening meal when the doorbell rang and upon answering it, I found two schoolgirls outside. They were aged about eight or nine, I guessed – I recognized one of them as Julie Mitchell whose parents lived in Aidensfield. The other was a school friend. 'We found this, Mr Rhea.' Julie held up a large iron key. 'Mum says we should bring it to you.'

'Goodness me!' I said. 'I think I know who's lost this! Where did you find it?'

'Under that big tree down near the river,' Julie said. 'We were playing down there just now and found it lying on the ground.'

I took it from her, weighed it in my hand, thanked them both profusely and said, 'I'll take it to the gentleman who I think has lost it. I think it might belong to Mr Greengrass, he's lost a key just like this one.'

Although I had finished work, I decided I should reunite Claude with his key as soon as possible – if indeed this belonged to him – and so I told Mary I was going for a quick walk along the village to the Greengrass ranch, but *en route*, decided to pay a quick visit to the tree in question. I knew the tree – it was a towering silver birch. And when I arrived, I realized the truth – the key had indeed been stolen from that guttering, but not by a human thief. High in the tree was the messy, untidy bulk of a nest, and a pair of magpies was hopping about in the branches, calling harshly at my intrusion beneath and I wondered if they had youngsters in the nest. Magpies are notorious for stealing bright objects and trinkets; they will even venture inside an open bedroom window if they catch sight of glistening objects on a dressing-table, and they carry them off to hide, often in their nests. I am sure many ladies have lost jewellery to thieving magpies. On this occasion, I think they had spotted the key in the guttering, probably with the sun glinting off it, and had carried it off then later dropped it as being unworthy of further interest.

When I arrived at Hagg Bottom, Claude was working on his damaged doorway and he pretended not to notice me. I am sure he thought I was going to ask some more apparently silly questions.

'What is it now? I'm busy!'

'I've got your key,' I announced, drawing it from my pocket and dangling it from my fingers. 'At least, I think it's yours. It was found by young Julie Mitchell and her schoolfriend. She handed it in.'

'See, I told you it had been nicked ... I bet those thieves were going to use it to rob me sometime, but with all this police activity, they've changed their minds. It's a good job I noticed it gone and reported it. Quick off the mark I am when folks do me an injustice.'

'It is yours, is it?' I needed confirmation for my records.

'Aye, it is.' He took it and examined it, then slipped it into his coat pocket. 'So what about the thief, then? Caught him, have you? Got him locked up?'

'He's been identified,' I smiled. 'Obviously, he's been visiting your buildings without you being aware of it, regularly, I'd say, and he's managed to slip away with this key without either you or David noticing. You'll have to be more observant, Claude – and more careful what you do with your precious belongings.'

'Careful? I'm always careful. I've had that key for years without once losing it till now.

'Even so, can I suggest you find another hiding place for your new keys?'

'No need,' he said. 'Like I said, I've got a spare. So, what are you going to do about this thief? Charge him I hope, teach him a lesson?'

'No, he won't be charged.'

'Pal of yours, is he?'

'No, but he's a local, a wily old bird by all accounts.'

'Well, I think you should make an example of him, bring him to court and let the papers tell the tale, how he plagued me and caused me expense and inconvenience by nicking my key and making me buy a new lock.'

'I can tell the newspapers if you like, Claude, but I think it's best to forget it now. You've got your key back, you've got a modern lock for your door and a nice new door post, and a spare key for David. I think that's enough.'

'Well, if it was me that had nicked summat, you'd soon be having me down to Ashfordly nick and charging me ... as the victim in this case, I demand an explanation!' And he stood up to glare at me.

'The thief is a magpie, Claude. Your key was found under its nest in that big silver birch near the river.'

'You're having me on, aren't you? You're enjoying this, making fun of my distress?' he glared.

'No, not at all. For me, the case is solved, I can delete it from our records. Maybe you might give young Julie a reward for handing it in, or of course, you might want to pop down to the river-bank to remonstrate personally with the thief. It would make a nice photo for the *Gazette* – you shouting "Devil, devil, I defy thee", or whatever you shout at magpies when you see them.'

'If I see it near my house again, I'll give it one for sorrow, so help me!' he laughed, then added, 'But thanks for bringing it back especially when you're off duty. And I will go and see young Julie with summat by way of thanks. Magpies ... pah! Do you know a magpie refused to go into the ark with Noah? Mebbe a good thing; it might have pinched all his keys for them stables, or wherever he kept all those animals. There'd have been a bit of a pong if he couldn't let 'em out for a run. Funny things, magpies are. My granny said they were witches in disguise!'

'Then be careful how you deal with it!' I laughed, and left him.

Chapter 6

Animals in the wild and on farms, as well as those kept as pets, regularly featured in my duties as a rural constable. On many occasions, I worked beside our local vets, especially if I had to deal with an animal injured in a road traffic accident, or one suspected of carrying a notifiable disease such as swine fever or foot-and-mouth, or even one which had been subjected to cruelty. The bulk of my duties where animals were involved came through my routine visits to farms, often to check stock movement registers, so consequently the proximity of animals was never a strange experience. Indeed, for any rural constable, it was to be expected.

Although one or two of the farms on my beat were wholly devoted to the growing of cereals or potatoes, with only a cat or two by way of livestock, many boasted herds of dairy or beef cattle, some specialized in sheep or pigs and another was the home of a famous breeder of heavy horses, Shires in particular. Several maintained a racehorse or two, some had goats and a few kept poultry. Most of the farms kept dogs and cats either as pets or working animals – some kept them as both – while other birds like geese, turkeys and ducks were commonplace.

High on the moors, of course, the sheep were not enclosed but roamed the heathery heights without restriction, knowing the boundaries of their own patch of moorland by an instinct inherited through many generations. These sheep were known as hefted, or in dialect, heeafed – it means they live on their own patch of moorland without the need for fencing or shepherds. Locals call them heeafed yows.

Being surrounded by so many animals meant that, even as a patrolling constable, one had to acquire some knowledge of their expected behaviour. It was important that I did not take unnecessary risks. One was always wary of bulls, for example, even if they appeared to be very docile in their fields or tethered by nose-rings in buildings. One had to remember that a cow, normally so peaceful and placid, could react dangerously if its calf appeared to be under threat (and a uniformed policeman on a noisy motorbike would have appeared rather strange to a protective mother cow). Mother sows could be very dangerous too, while a lot of dogs seemed to dislike people in dark uniforms. For some reason, they like to attack what are now called uniformed postal delivery operatives – we called them postmen. In spite of the overall need for constant general caution, I knew there were times I could walk through a field of sheep, cattle or horses without the risk of trouble, while hens scattered as I patrolled through them, geese hissed, ducks quacked and pigs grunted.

Having spent all my life in the countryside, I thought I could cope with, or anticipate, almost any situation so far as animals were concerned. There was one simple piece of overriding advice – if danger looks likely in the presence of an animal, maintain your distance, preferably behind a gate or wall. Don't antagonize the creature; don't try to appease it by patting it on the head; don't make any sudden movements; don't attempt to walk behind it, and if it has youngsters, don't try to make friends with them. There are exceptions of course – some of the moorland sheep in places like Goathland are so tame they will attempt to climb into cars in the search of food.

Even if its intention is friendly, a full grown sheep with a fine set of horns can terrify children and might even cause an injury, however unintentionally. It is not wise to encourage them to take titbits, just as it is not wise to encourage ducks, coots and water hens to join you in the car by feeding them near a village pond. When visiting houses, one was always wary of territorial dogs, and even geese could stage a frightening scene if they felt one was trespassing upon their ground. For all this acquired knowledge and experience, however, I once found myself having some difficulty coping with hens. It came at a time when animal-loving protesters were campaigning against the practice of rearing hens in deep-litter houses and in battery units.

This was not a new development within the agricultural world, but it was one which was growing in popularity due to the increasing demand for more food which had to be produced quickly and cheaply. Instead of hens running free around the farm or smallholding, they were kept in long low sheds, usually built of wood, where they were expected to produce lots of eggs, or alternatively to be fattened for slaughter – or both. In many cases, hens were slaughtered to be used as human food after the end of their egg-laying life. During the early stages of this kind of intensive farming, which began in the late 1940s, the hens ran around the floors of large specially-constructed windowless buildings. Those floors were covered in some two feet (60 cm or so) of straw and the system was known as deep litter. The hens ate and slept in these buildings – they never went outside and thus never knew the joy of scratching raw earth, breathing fresh air, and running across the road in front of motor vehicles. In such conditions, it did not take poultry owners long to realize that the natural egg-laying timetable of a hen could be extended quite simply by illuminating those gigantic hen houses and, if necessary, adding temp-erature control, humidity and ventilation, with automatic feeding and a constant sup-ply of fresh water. Normally, a hen would begin laying towards the end of winter and continue throughout the spring, summer and autumn. Some farmers claimed their birds laid eggs on some 300 days out of the year's 365, but 150 was a more realistic figure.

The success of this system, and the ever-increasing demand for cheaper food, led to the idea that the birds need not run around deep-litter floors. Instead, they could be kept in individual wire-mesh cages, stacked one on top of the other, inside buildings with artificial conditions to woo them into laying yet more eggs. In addition, birds could be specially bred for slaughter, being reared intensively and then killed after some eleven weeks or so.

Tiers of wire cages were stacked in long rows. The hens received water from a little gutter which passed in front of their cages and they obtained their food from a conveyor belt. The cages were so small that a hen could barely turn around; the floor was of wire mesh too, so there was no nesting material and it was said that when the hens became bored with this existence, they began to peck themselves, thus severely injuring their own bodies. Indeed, some were already doing this in the deep-litter system, and some hens were fitted with little devices on their beaks to prevent them pecking one another, or injuring themselves.

Artificial lighting was kept burning day and night, and temperature control was used in winter to confuse the hens into being unable to distinguish night from day, or summer from winter, thus producing more eggs. In spite of some poultry farmers doing their best to make the birds' lives as comfortable as possible, many of the less-well run establishments appeared to have no thought for the well-being of the hens. During my time at Aidensfield, some 99 per cent of the nation's broiler chickens were kept in such conditions, with individual flocks numbering up to 100,000 birds in some cases. Even fairly modest flocks could number anywhere between 8,000 and 17,000 birds. Eighty per cent of egg-laying birds were kept in wire cages in rows of battery houses; only 5 per cent were free-range, the remainder being reared in deep-litter houses. For the poultry farmer, it was very successful, because it kept labour costs down while production was high.

Although this system allowed the mass production of cheap food – something which aided the growth of supermarkets and undoubtedly helped to feed the nation – it was repeatedly criticized by bird and animal lovers. This led to demonstrations, placard waving and even attacks on poultry units and the farmers themselves.

This is where the police entered the story. The 1960s was a decade of protests, some of them silly with strong but unworkable political motivation, and they ranged from campaigns to Ban-The-Bomb to those designed to bring an end to police brutality. Indeed, almost any cause, national, international or local, could produce a banner-waving, loud-voiced and sometimes violent demonstration. For some, protesting had almost become a way of life in the 1960s. It must be said that most of the demos were undertaken by earnest young people who wished for nothing more than a peaceful means of highlighting their very genuine concerns. But such innocents rarely considered the impact of what the police called rent-a-mob. This was a loosely knit, highly mobile bunch of troublemakers, who often lived on social security, and who regarded any kind of demonstration as a form of universal sport in which they could injure police officers, damage property, insult bystanders and create all manner of civil disturbance under the guise of fighting for freedom and democracy.

Upon learning about the date and venue of a demonstration of any kind, they would turn up in large numbers to create untold havoc, then leave as quickly as they arrived. Once their actions had achieved the success they desired, they abandoned the genuine protesters who were then left to explain things and pay the cost of the damage and vandalism, either through court or by other means. No demonstration, however small and localized, was free from the attentions of rent-a-mob. One of their known techniques, especially during the large demonstrations in London, was to smear their faces with tomato ketchup, contrive to get their photographs taken by the Press and then claim the police had assaulted them and drawn blood. They would also slash police horses, try to blind them and throw marbles under their hooves – and they committed all manner of even worse underhand methods, invariably beyond the sight of cameras and witnesses.

And so it was, when police intelligence discovered that well-meaning hen lovers were going to wave banners outside an unidentified battery-type chicken farm somewhere in England this coming autumn, there would have to be contingency plans to cope with the possible presence of seasoned, skilful troublemakers. Thanks to a good intelligence network and infiltration of the worst of the subversive organizations, it was often known in advance when and where troublemakers were intending to join a protest. It was even known which of them would attend a particular demonstration. In this case, however, it was not known which chicken farm was to be the focus of their attention. It might be one at Aidensfield, or there again, it could be one in Kent, Cornwall or Cumberland – as the demonstrators began to grow more cautious in revealing their plans, we understood they were learning to be devious and cunning. Perhaps they hoped to fool the police, but, they should have been avoiding the trouble-makers who pretended to support them.

Against this background, therefore, along with other rural policemen, and with Sergeant Craddock in attendance, I was called to a meeting in Ashfordly police station where we were addressed by a member of the Special Branch. We were supplied with details of the anticipated action by militants, and furnished with photographs of the suspected rural terrorists as well as the genuine demonstrators. It was stressed that the precise target was, at this stage, unknown, but each of us was asked to maintain a watching brief on the poultry units on our patch, and to report any sightings of possible trouble-makers or their vehicles.

When the time came for any questions, I asked, 'Can we alert the poultry farmers in question? It might help if they could look at these photographs and tell us if they've seen any of these people wandering about near their premises.'

'We must be careful not to create unnecessary and widespread alarm,' said the Special Branch officer. 'Our general practice is to maintain as much secrecy as possible ahead of a demonstration, usually without the targets realizing they are a target. One reason is because they often have contacts within target organizations. But these chicken farmers are solitary people, I can't see them, or anyone employed by them, being in league with militant left-wingers. We're talking here of an attempt to destroy a small part of capitalism; that's the aim of rent-a-mob, not the aim of the genuine demonstrators, so I see no harm in alerting the poultry owners, provided they don't take the law into their own hands by shooting trespassers or setting man-traps! We want things to appear as normal as possible – we want to arrest some of these yobs if we can, with enough evidence to convict them. I stress it's not the peaceful demonstrators we're after. And, in response to PC Rhea's question, yes, it would be helpful if the farmers could inform us of anyone pretending to be a rambler, bird-watcher, poultry-food salesman or whatever, while making a recce of the premises.'

We were then briefed on the action we should take from this stage onwards, and were told of the contingency plans through which additional officers and vehicles could be mustered at short notice, provided the intelligence was accurate, and a genuine threat was seen as imminent.

After more questions, and some dreadful examples of the methods used by left-wing militants to discredit the police, the meeting concluded and we all went home. It made me both thoughtful and angry about the subversive and illegal methods used by unscrupulous activists and I decided there was no time to waste. The following day I opted to visit the two chicken farms on my patch, still astonished that one of our local hen houses – or poultry unit to be more precise – could become the centre of attention in a violent demo of some kind. Whilst I could understand the earnest concern of animal lovers in staging a peaceful demonstration of banner waving and slogan shouting, I could not believe that left-wingers would join them in an attempt to destroy a small local business, probably by violent means. Surely, I reasoned, genuine bird lovers would not wish to harm the poultry? But my task was not to ponder such things – it was not to suppress the demonstration either because peaceful demonstrations are part of our democracy, but my duty was to prevent a breach of the peace and to preserve life and property. That was always our role, even if some claimed otherwise.

And so it was that, against this background, I embarked upon my poultry-shed patrol. My beat contained two poultry farms, each with three huge but windowless units, and at that stage I had no idea which, if any, were deep-litter houses and which contained hens in batteries. I had never had reason to enter either of the units although I had regularly called upon their respective owners. One unit was sited on a hill-top above the river at Elsinby – not surprisingly called Riverview Farm – and the other was one of the enterprises of Crampton Estate.

In the latter case, the three poultry sheds of the Crampton unit were situated at the western end of that village, on land adjoining Home Farm. The poultry keeper for Crampton Estate was a wartime Polish refugee called Stefan Oltstzyn, while the Elsinby farm was owned by Ken Southwell and his wife, Gillian. Dealing with Ken and Gillian Southwell would not be difficult, but in the case of Crampton Estate there would be an element of bureaucracy to overcome. To whom should I speak about my concerns? Stefan, an employee with broken English, or the estate manager, or even Lord Crampton himself?

Taking the easy option, I decided I'd begin with Ken and Gillian. It was a beautiful sunny and slightly breezy day in October, with the bronze, yellow and red colours of the maturing trees painting a stunning backcloth along my short journey to Elsinby. The river-bank trees which surrounded the village were a delight – the slender and delicate branches of graceful silver birches swayed above sturdy alders while here and there, a dark conifer would rise among them, as if defying the onset of autumn by stubbornly remaining green. The oaks were clinging to their leaves while the ash trees had delivered theirs to the earth, and the sycamores were casting their foliage in small clouds with each puff of wind. Just across the bridge, I turned right

191

and drove up the steeply sloping track with the farmhouse, its outbuildings and chicken sheds on the summit. The sheds stood a couple of hundred yards beyond the complex of farm buildings and so I parked my Mini-van on the concrete beside the back door of the house, climbed out and then wondered whether or not to ring the bell or go immediately to the chicken sheds.

I could hear music and calculated it was emanating from the sheds – inside, it must sound quite loud and I wondered if listening to music made the chickens happier, but guessed it would be Ken entertaining himself as he worked at some chore, like cleaning them out or collecting eggs. My problem about whether to disturb him was solved by the appearance of Gillian in the doorway; she'd heard the arrival of my van. A well-built lady of ample proportions in her mid-forties, she had a head of fine auburn hair, heavy tortoiseshell-rimmed spectacles and a round, cheerful face with a ready smile. She waved at me then beckoned me to go into the house – I knew coffee would be offered, and perhaps a slice of apple pie or fruit cake. Irresistible! I followed her into the kitchen when she said, 'That's good timing, Mr Rhea. You must have smelt it, I've just called Ken.'

'I was on my way to see him,' I told her.

'You wouldn't be able to get into the sheds,' she informed me. 'But he'll be here in a minute or two for his coffee. I've rung him.'

'Rung him?'

'He locks himself in when he's working with the chickens,' she smiled. 'To stop folks opening the doors. We've a telephone extension in there, I ring it when it's coffee or lunch time.'

'It sounds like prison to me!' I laughed, sitting on a chair which she had eased out for me at the table.

'The chickens mustn't be disturbed,' she said. 'If someone walks in unexpectedly, they all start flapping and squawking and it affects their performance – they lay fewer eggs and that costs money.'

'Temperamental, are they?' I asked.

'Like prima donnas!' she laughed, busying herself with coffee and finding some chunks of cake. 'The slightest interruption to their routine has a terrible effect on them.'

'So you'll not be pleased when jets hurtle across these hills?'

'No, we've had words with the RAF, but there's not a lot they can do. They promised to fly as far away as possible from us, but there's always planes about these skies. That's why we have the music; it's very loud inside those sheds.'

'Music?' I smiled.

'Music and loud talk on the radio. A constant noise is what we want. It drowns all external sounds, even the louder ones, and it means we can go about our normal business with noisy machinery or tractors and so forth, without worrying how it will affect the hens. The radio plays all the time so they're used to it, but they seem to prefer music to chatter. I'm not sure whether it makes a real difference, but it keeps us entertained if we're working in there.'

'So fireworks on Bonfire Night, aircraft hurtling across the moors, motor bikes revving up and so on, have no effect on your hens?'

'Such noises don't seem to bother them while the radio's playing. If we switch it off, they can cope with the silence, but any sudden noise, even someone knocking on their door or kicking a bucket over will startle them and cause them to panic. And if some hens stop laying, they might never start again.'

'I've seen farmyard hens run in mass panic

whenever I've ridden near them on my motor bike!'

'Exactly. We daren't risk that kind of panic in our sheds, so it's music while you work for all our hens, Mr Rhea. Luckily, we can't hear it down here at the house and it's well away from the cattle sheds.'

'Well, that's something I've learned!' I laughed, and then the door opened and in strode Ken Southwell.

'Hello, Nick, I saw your van. Summat wrong, or is this just a routine call?'

Slightly older than his wife, he was a powerfully built man with dark hair but balding on his crown, with grey eyes and a round, ruddy face which hadn't seen a razor for a few days. As always, he looked cheerful and content as he removed his flat cap and tan-coloured dustcoat and hung it behind the door.

'It's a visit with a special message,' I said as he sat opposite. Gillian pricked up her ears at this and joined us. I then told them about the intelligence we had received and said all rural police officers would be calling at poultry farms to alert the owners to a possible visit from demonstrators.

I showed them the photographs of both the genuine and rogue demonstrators, asking that if they spotted anyone of their description lingering near their premises, possibly to survey the layout or work out a plan of attack, to inform us and obtain details of things like car registration numbers, detailed descriptions of the visitors and so forth.

'We're a fair distance from the road,' Ken pointed out. 'I thought demonstrators weren't allowed on private premises? There's no public right of way along that lane of mine and luckily, we've no public footpaths through our land.'

'The genuine protestors will adhere to that policy, I'm sure, but I can't speak for the lawbreaking elements who might join them or try to influence them.'

'Well, if those lunatics trespass on my land, I'll have a shock waiting them, I can tell you!'

'I don't want to know about that,' I told him, reminding him that he must not take the law into his own hands by shooting them, laying traps and so forth.

'I know all about that, Nick,' he assured me. 'And I know I owe a duty of care to trespassers, but it doesn't stop me protecting my own livestock in the way I feel right at the time. A bit of farmyard muck sprayed over them accidentally by a passing muck-spreader isn't a bad start! It's often enough to see 'em off! But thanks for the warning, we'll keep our eyes open, won't we, Gillian?'

I remained for a further fifteen minutes or so, enjoying the coffee, the cake and the banter, and then took my leave.

Ken said, 'You've not seen my set-up, have you, Nick? If you're keeping an eye open for townie louts and vandals who are brave enough to tackle creatures as dangerous or as savage as hens, you'd better see just what goes on inside those sheds.'

Donning his dustcoat and cap, he led me towards one of the sheds and, as we approached, the music grew louder and louder; when he arrived at the outer door, he banged on it, gently at first and then increasingly louder, shouting at me, 'This gets 'em used to the idea that summat's going to happen! They don't like sudden shocks. Inside here there's a lobby. I'll give you a smock and a cap; hens don't like things looking different but two of us looking alike doesn't alarm 'em...'

He had a combination lock on the outer door into which he pressed a series of numbers and this released the outer door and we went inside. As I donned my outfit in the lobby, he rattled the inner door several times with his fist and now I knew why; then he gave me a pair of ear-muffs of the kind used by people taking part in indoor rifle and pistol shooting and opened the door. Inside, the building was illuminated with artificial light and the heat was higher than the temperature out of doors. The stench was appalling, but although he did not notice it, it almost took my breath away. Ahead of me were thousands and thousands of hens in wire cages, all clucking and pecking and drinking. Birds, I am assured, have no sense of smell! They took absolutely no notice of us as we walked down the lines, with me noting the automatic feeders, water system, egg collection and dirt removal, and with Ken using hand signals to highlight some of the systems.

I must admit I did not like to see birds enclosed like this and yet I could see that everything had been done to make the birds as comfortable as possible. The sheer number of birds in each shed made me realize that if their egg-laying was interrupted and, say, 25 per cent of them stopped laying for just one day, then it meant a shortage of considerable proportions. Ken explained how he ran one cockerel to every ten hens, but some older cocks were liable to get arthritis which reduced their abilities and consequently reduced the hatchability of the eggs. If a cock was defective, it had to be replaced, but the hens would only accept their new beau if the previous champion had gone. If he remained, they would ignore the new chap!

After my brief tour, he led me outside and said he was sure I now knew the kind of atmosphere necessary for the birds to produce their best, adding that all poultry keepers adopted similar devices. They made good use of locked doors, continuous noise, no sudden arrivals or changes in routine, no different working garments – in fact, nothing which would startle or alarm the thousands of hens in confinement. I thanked him and said I was now heading for Crampton Estate's poultry unit on a like mission.

'You'll find it's just like this,' he smiled. 'Well away from the road, well secured and with all the necessary ingredients to keep the birds happy. I doubt any demonstrators will get near any of our units, but if they do, they'll have to make one hell of a racket to produce any effect! And all the doors are locked, so they can't gain entry to frighten the birds. But we'll keep our eyes peeled for troublemakers, Nick.'

'And I'll keep you informed of developments,' I assured him, before driving off to Crampton.

As I drove across the hills, I decided I would present my information to Crampton's estate manager who could then decide how and when to notify Lord Crampton, and how to deal with Stefan Oltstzyn and his poultry unit. As I motored, I reflected on how much I had learned about hens and hen psychology. But thinking of all the possible underhand methods that might be used by the demonstrators, it only really needed one person to gain entry to a poultry unit, then switch off the radio, run about in a gaudy coat and shout 'boo!'

If such tactics continued over a period, it would soon make the owner bankrupt – but true hen lovers would never do such a frightful thing to defenceless chickens, although, I suppose, some demonstrators might be capable of saying boo to a goose.

While one was required to exercise great tenderness and gentle behaviour in the presence of nervous battery chickens, I was soon to discover that a similar approach was needed when dealing with a massive dog called Cyclops. Cyclops was well-named. He was a Pyrenean mountain dog, a huge, white-coated animal whose fur contained very faint biscuit-coloured markings, but his chief identifying feature was that he had only one eye, hence his name. Like the fabled Cyclops, this dog was a giant among his fellows, but he was not invincible because he had lost his left eye in a road accident while a pup. It was rumoured he'd tried to chase off a mobile crane, with little success, but something heavy had fallen from the vehicle and hit him as he had pursued it along the street.

Larger than a St Bernard when fully grown, the Pyrenean mountain dog is noted for its abilities to guard most things. It was used centuries ago to protect flocks of sheep in the Pyrenean mountains; it could see off wolves and bears which means it is no wimp. It was also used as a dog of war, when it went into battle wearing a spiked collar, and of course, it found lots of work as a general guard dog, not only in the Pyrenees but throughout the world, guarding everything from famous people to famous and valuable things. In fairly recent times, it has been used as a guide dog, where it is especially useful in mountainous regions, but for all its massive size and historic role as a guardian, it is usually friendly and affable in the domestic situation, with an appearance not unlike an outsize light-coated golden retriever.

Cyclops was such a dog, but he was not a resident of Aidensfield, however. He was a visitor. His owner was Miss Kathleen Hollins, aged forty-five or thereabouts, who was a lecturer at Leeds University and who had been invited to travel overseas on a geography scholarship of some kind. The term of the scholarship was one year during which she had to travel within the southern hemisphere and learn something of its topography so that it would enhance her work when she returned to England. She could not take Cyclops with her and did not want to place him in a dogs' home for such a long period, nor did she even contemplate having him put to sleep. After all, he was only six years old, full of life and a wonderful companion for her – furthermore, I was to learn, he was a very capable guardian of her bungalow on the outskirts of Harrogate. Trespassing cats, dogs, foxes, housebreakers, burglars and door-to-door salesmen stood no chance against this most powerful of protectors. His deep bark alone was enough to send most unwanted visitors scurrying off, and if this failed to impress, then a growl or snarl or two provided an added impetus to vacate the premises with commendable speed.

Kathleen had a sister called Doreen who was also unmarried. Doreen Hollins lived in Aidensfield, her home being a lovely detached cottage along Elsinby Road. Facing south, it had ivy on the walls, an archway over the door covered with honeysuckle and a large garden which she tended meticulously. Doreen was a freelance music teacher who would bring pupils into her home where she taught them how to play the piano, or she would visit them in their own homes to do likewise; in addition, she taught music part-time in one or two of the local public schools. She taught both children and adults, and, I knew, she had a wonderful record of successes.

When Kathleen received her news of the scholarship, her first thoughts were for Cyclops – what on earth could be done with him? And then she remembered her sister in Aidensfield, an amenable lady who had once kept a Yorkshire terrier and who therefore knew a bit about dog keeping. Kathleen put her proposal to Doreen and after spending an entire weekend contemplating such a large visitor to her home, Doreen eventually agreed. Cyclops could become her lodger.

Kathleen brought him from Harrogate one Friday evening in August and remained on the premises until the following Monday morning so that Cyclops would become accustomed to the house and its environs, and, in time, accustomed to Doreen. The weekend was a surprising success with Cyclops apparently realizing that this was to be his new abode. Alone with Doreen on some early test outings, he went for walks on the nearby moors and in the woods, he explored fields and river-banks, and he made friends with some of the children who came to Doreen for music lessons. Then, when Kathleen left on the Monday, to prepare for her trip overseas, Cyclops flopped down on the mat before the fire and appeared to know that here he would remain for some considerable time. He became friendly with Doreen and she could manage him with surprising ease. I would often see them out for walks, which was how I first encountered Cyclops, and I could see he was happy with his temporary mistress. As the days passed, he fussed over her students, especially the children, and they all fussed over him, so that in a very short time he was accepted as part of the village, and a fascinating asset to Doreen's career. The arrangement had worked out surprisingly well and everyone who met Cyclops thought he was wonderful.

Then, after a few weeks of this blissful situation, I received a worried phone call from Doreen.

'Mr Rhea, I don't know what to do. Cyclops is misbehaving and I can't do a thing with him; he growls at me all the time and I don't know who to ask for help. So I rang you. I thought the police could deal with anything.'

'Growls at you? So where are you?' I asked, thinking he might have banished her from the happy home.

'I'm at home,' she said. 'And he's in the sitting-room, in an easy chair. He won't get out, Mr Rhea, he sits in the chair and growls every time I go near him.'

'He's claimed the chair, you mean?'

'Yes, I think so. He's not done it before, not the whole time he's been here; he always sleeps on the floor in the kitchen; he's got his own clip rug.'

'So how long has he been there? In the chair?'

'Since yesterday tea-time,' she said. 'I had a pupil in my music-room until five and when she'd gone, there he was, sitting up in the chair as if he owned it. I went to pat him and to tell him to get down, but he just growled at me and refused to move. I thought he might come down for his food and water, which he did, but the minute I went anywhere near the chair, he jumped back up and growled at me. He won't let me anywhere near it, Mr Rhea. He's guarding that chair as if he owns it. He'll leave it if I am busy elsewhere, but the moment I go anywhere near it, he leaps up and growls at me. But once he gets out of it, he's as friendly as usual.'

'So what about his toilet routine?' I had to ask.

'Oh, he's done his jobs all right. When I called him to go out for walkies, he came straight away and followed me through the wood, but the minute we got back home, he went straight to the chair and leapt into it. I mean, Mr Rhea, he's so huge he can hardly get into it, but he squats there like a big bear, leaning against the backrest and looking most uncomfortable, but he refuses to leave it, except for emergencies. I can't use it now and it's my favourite chair, Mr

Rhea. I can't do with him dominating it like that.'

'Are they very territorial animals, these mountain dogs?' I asked.

'No more than any other,' she responded. 'I know some dogs like to be dominant but he seems determined to keep me away from my own chair, and I can't really have that in my own home.'

'Are you in touch with your sister?' was my next question. 'She might know what to do.'

'No, she's deep in some jungle, miles away from a telephone, and I can't even get a letter to her, not until the end of the month. That's three weeks away.'

'I'll come and have a look at Cyclops,' I said. 'But I can't promise it will do any good.'

'I thought you might have experts in the police, dog handlers and people like that, doggy people who know about these things.'

'We do have dog handlers but I'm not sure they know how to get a determined Pyrenean mountain dog out of a chair,' I said. 'But I'll come and introduce myself to Cyclops and we'll see what happens.'

'I really would appreciate that,' she said.

When I rang her door bell, I heard Cyclops bark somewhere inside the house but did not regard that as a threat; after all, Doreen Hollins had a regular procession of visitors to her home and so the dog would be accustomed to such noises.

Smiling her gratitude, she took me into the kitchen and said, 'It is so kind of you to help me like this, Mr Rhea; really I didn't know who to turn to.'

And with that, a large light-coloured shape pushed open the inner door and I saw Cyclops watching me with his single eye. He came in, sniffed at me, wagged his tail briskly and so I patted him and said, 'Hello Cyclops.'

He wagged his tail again then turned around and left.

'He seems quite normal to me,' I felt compelled to observe.

'Just you see what he does if you go near his chair,' she smiled.

I noticed that she referred to 'his' chair; if the dog was seeking to claim the furniture as his very own, it almost looked as if he had succeeded and so I decided I must observe this phenomenon at first hand. Miss Hollins escorted me into the lounge where Cyclops was sprawled across the hearth rug but the minute we entered the room, the huge animal rose to his feet, crossed to the chair and leapt into it, settling down in what had become the most comfortable position, leaning against the upright with his rear legs curled up on the cushion and his front legs on the arm. Then he snarled, just once, baring his teeth as he glared at us.

'Come along, Cyclops,' said Miss Hollins. 'Come down at once ... you naughty dog...'

As she made a pretend move to go closer, Cyclops reacted with a snarl or two and then some loud barks of warning.

'All right, Cyclops,' I said. 'I get the message,' and we left the room.

Miss Hollins explained that that was how he reacted the entire time; if pupils came for lessons, he was friendly and approachable anywhere in the house or grounds, except within range of 'his' chair. I tried to learn a little more about his life in Harrogate, but Miss Hollins couldn't help, except to say that whenever she had visited her sister, Cyclops had never shown such tendencies. He'd always been most friendly although he would bark if strangers came to the house, or if he heard unfamiliar noises. My very amateurish efforts at dog psychiatry produced no useful information or guidance and I was reminded of the old joke about the man who came home from the pet shop with a giant gorilla. It stood about fifteen feet (about 4.5 metres) tall, and his wife said, 'Where is he going to sleep?'

'Anywhere he damn well pleases,' was the response.

It was something like that with Cyclops. Back in the kitchen, I had to express my inability to think of any positive means of dealing with the stubborn dog, but I did not want Miss Hollins to think I was doing nothing.

'I think we'll have to let him do as he pleases for the time being,' I told her. 'Either he'll get sick of sitting in that chair – it looks most uncomfortable – or he will decide it is not really the place to spend all his free time. Or else you could tempt him away on a walk and then put him in a dogs' home for a few days in the hope he might forget about the chair.'

'Oh, I couldn't do that to him, Mr Rhea, he'd be most unhappy and besides, I promised Kathleen I would never do that ... not poor Cyclops.'

'Look,' I said, 'I have a very good friend who is one of our best dog trainers. I'll give him a ring tonight and see if he can help. He's in the Police Dog Section but I'm not sure what his duties are, so it might take time for me to catch him, but that's all I can promise. He's very good with dogs of all kinds, Alsatians especially. I'll see if he has any ideas.'

'Would you? I'd be very grateful. I think, in the meantime, I'll have to let Cyclops continue to occupy his territory!'

'I can't see any alternative,' I had to admit.

That evening, I rang my friend Colin who happened to be off duty and at home, and he listened to the tale with evident interest. After what I hoped was a factual account from me, he said, 'I've not much experience with Pyrenean mountain dogs, but it seems to me he's guarding the chair. I don't think this is a territorial claim of any kind; he'll regard the house and grounds as his territory now and he'll guard that against invaders if he has to – the whole house I mean – so I think his attachment to the chair is because he's decided to guard something – perhaps the chair itself or something in it, but if you ask me why he's suddenly decided to do that, I have no idea. But his behaviour does suggest he's reverting to his natural instinct of being a guard dog so far as the chair is concerned.'

'Perhaps Miss Hollins has left something in her chair that he's taken to?'

'I don't think he would guard anything without being given some kind of order or signal, something he understands. He wouldn't guard something without reason. This kind of stubborn behaviour suggests he's obeying an order of some kind. To be honest, Nick, I don't think a dog of that size would sit in an armchair out of choice!'

'So what can you suggest?' I put to him.

'Have another word with the lady, see if she can remember doing anything that might have been interpreted as an order by the dog. I'll give you an example. A friend of mine once owned a yellow labrador and it was trained to sit if he raised his right hand with the palm facing the dog. One day, he was out with his dog and met a colleague; during their conversation he raised his hand in that very gesture to emphasize a point, and the dog promptly sat down without the owner realizing. The two men walked off together with my friend still not realizing he'd ordered Paddy, his labrador, to sit, and the dog continued to sit there. They'd walked two miles before they realized Paddy wasn't with them. They had to retrace their steps and found the unhappy dog still sitting as he'd been ordered, however unwittingly the order had been given.'

'So you think Miss Hollins has unwittingly ordered the dog to guard the chair?'

'Probably not Miss Hollins,' said Colin. 'Someone else. If she had issued the order, she's the only person who can cancel it. I don't think the big dog would growl at her if she was the person who had issued the order.'

'So he could be obeying someone else's order?' I asked.

'I think so. There must be some key word or signal which was used by your friend's sister while she was looking after the dog, and I think someone's used the same word or sign without realizing. So has anyone else been in the house?'

'She's a music teacher,' I said. 'Pupils come regularly for lessons. And I guess she has neighbours popping in.'

'All I can suggest, Nick, is that you go back to Miss Hollins to see who's been to the house, especially in the time immediately before the dog began his vigil, and then ask that visitor if he or she might have unwittingly ordered the dog to guard something.'

I thanked him for his help and so that same evening, I decided to walk down to Miss Hollins's house to see if Colin's theory held any promise of release for her. During the walk, I recalled her first conversation with me about Cyclops; she said she'd emerged from her music-room at five one evening after a lesson with a pupil, and that's when she'd first found Cyclops in the chair. As I arrived at the house, I wondered if that pupil, a girl if I remembered correctly, had unwittingly given an order to the dog. If so, it would be probably be a week from that time before she returned...

As usual, the ring of the door bell produced a loud bark within and when Miss Hollins answered, Cyclops was at her side, wagging his tail, sniffing at me and being completely friendly.

As she led me into the lounge, he bolted ahead and leapt into his chair to adopt his usual guard-like position, complete with a snarl of warning not to venture too close. Miss Hollins had meanwhile rearranged the chairs so that she could settle down at a distance from the dog, and so when we sat at the other end of the lounge, Cyclops appeared to accept this. As we discussed our business, he glared at us with his single eye.

I explained Colin's theory and she said, 'Yes, I did have a pupil just before he started all this nonsense. A twelve-year-old girl,

Alison Green from Elsinby; she comes once a week.'

'Could she have left something in that chair?' I asked.

'It's very possible, Mr Rhea, my pupils are always leaving things behind; they treat the place as their own, throwing scarves and hats on to the chairs, leaving satchels behind if they come straight from school, that sort of thing. Sometimes they come back for them, and sometimes, if it's not urgent, they collect their belongings the following week.'

'I can understand that, but it's hardly likely she would throw something down in your favourite chair, is it?'

'Ah!' I seemed to have sparked off her memory. 'Ah, yes. I think I've got it. It would not be anything of hers. Her mother promised to let me have a magazine with a knitting pattern in it ... yes, that's it, Mr Rhea. It was *Woman's Weekly*. When Alison arrived, she was carrying the magazine ... I remember now. Cyclops came and sniffed it, and I told Alison to pop it on to my chair, then I'd be sure to find it.'

'So she must have said something to Cyclops?'

'If she did, I've no idea what!' laughed Miss Hollins. 'So you mean that silly dog has been guarding my *Woman's Weekly* all this time? As a matter of fact, I wondered what I'd done with it!'

'There's only one way to find out,' I said, 'and that's to get Alison here to cancel the order to Cyclops – unless you want to wait until she comes for her next lesson!'

Doreen rang Alison's parents – they were good friends and Mrs Green said she had to pop across to Aidensfield to deliver some eggs to a friend, so she could come straight away and bring Alison with her. It would take about twenty minutes, she said, and so I opted to wait to see the outcome of this dilemma. Alison was a tall, bonny young girl with dark hair and when she came in, she looked alarmed at my presence, wondering if she'd done something wrong, but was soon laughing as we explained the problem.

'I put it in your chair like you said, Miss Hollins,' she told us.

'And what was Cyclops doing?' I asked.

'Well, he was making a fuss and sniffing about and wagging his tail, and when I put the magazine on the chair, he jumped in and sat on it. He looked really stupid, sat there like a big bear!'

'Did you say anything to him?' asked Miss Hollins.

'I might have said something like "Guard it!", but it was a joke, just because he was sitting on it. We tell our dog at home to guard things as well, but he doesn't take any notice.'

'I think we need to see what reaction Cyclops gives to Alison,' I suggested and so we trooped into the lounge. At the sound of our approach, Cyclops leapt into the chair to resume his duties, but this time, when he saw Alison he did not snarl or growl, but wagged his tail as best he could in the cramped conditions.

'Good dog, Cyclops,' said Alison, and with that simple thank you, the giant dog came down from the chair and fussed about Alison who patted him and said, 'Good dog, what a good dog...'

'Well, I'll be blowed!' said Miss Hollins.

'Only Alison could have got that result. But go towards the chair and see what happens, Miss Hollins,' I suggested, not entirely with confidence. Bravely, I thought, she went towards the chair and Cyclops followed, but this time he did not growl or snarl, but wagged his enormous tail as she picked up a very crumpled and sat-upon copy of *Woman's Weekly*.

'Good dog,' Miss Hollins said. 'What a

good dog!'

And the huge animal strutted around the room, his vigorously wagging tail threatening to demolish the ornaments on the shelves and the flowers on the coffee table, his duty now over. But he had done very well indeed; he had performed his important task with credit and determination, and so I said, 'Does he get treats?'

'He loves chocolate biscuits,' said Miss Hollins.

'Then I think he's earned one,' I suggested. 'He has performed his task with diligence and devotion well beyond the normal call of duty. A chocolate biscuit is a good reward, I think. How about you, Cyclops?'

And as he wagged his tail, I was sure I saw that big single eye wink at Alison.

Chapter 7

Having submitted my application to appear before the promotion board, I received a memo to say it would be held six months hence on Wednesday 25 October at police headquarters where my presence would be required at 11.30 a.m. I had to be dressed in my best uniform and I knew I must ensure I had a decent hair cut, that my trousers were neatly pressed with sharp creases, that my uniform was brushed clean and that my boots were polished so that I could see my face in the toecap. I was also told the board would comprise the chief constable, the deputy chief constable, the superintendent from my own division and two other super-intendents from other divisions of the Force. I would be interviewed by them for half an hour or so, and afterwards the result would be relayed to me by letter. I thought six months' notice was a long time, but later discovered this was done for two reasons – first to allow the candidates to prepare well in advance, and second, to allow for the vagaries of police duties, court appearances, annual leave and so forth, thus giving the candidates ample time to avoid a conflict of commitments.

Promotion boards were a fairly recent innovation within our Force; hitherto, promotion depended entirely upon one's performance (albeit having passed the requisite examinations) and it was not, as members of the public often thought, the result of making a good or spectacular arrest, or having an uncle in high places. Promotion had necessarily to be on merit and an officer won promotion, not always for what he or she had achieved, but for what he or she was expected to achieve in that higher rank.

Furthermore, such a promotion was ultimately for the benefit of the Force and consequently for the benefit of the general public. In addition to these considerations, there was always the overriding fact that there was an established number of posts within the service – and that meant there was also a limited number of vacancies for sergeants. It followed that a constable could not expect promotion until a vacancy occurred, and that might take some time. This period of waiting produced an expression that promotions were a means of filling dead men's shoes but that was not entirely true within the service. Although some sergeants were promoted to inspector, those who failed to achieve that goal had to retire at the age of fifty-five, unless they could secure an extension of service of, say, another year. There had to be a very good reason for the granting of such an extension and, of course, the candidate had to be physically and mentally fit.

In a numerically small force like the North Riding Constabulary, with fewer than 600 police personnel at that time, vacancies for any rank did not occur very frequently which in reality meant most constables did not win that first step up the ladder of promotion until they had completed some twelve years' service or more. Later, accelerated promotion schemes were introduced, but for most of us that was the normal situation. If it meant that promotion came slowly, it ensured that when a constable eventually attained the rank of sergeant, he had a wealth of valuable practical experience – and confidence – upon which he could draw. In dealing with members of the public, and the huge variety of incidents they create, then such experience is vital.

The introduction of promotion boards meant that, to some extent, the furtherance of one's career was now the responsibility of the individuals concerned; hitherto, hopefuls had to await the decision of some unseen higher authority who nominated candidates and discussed them behind closed doors. Prior to promotion boards, promotion came as a nice surprise – but now the situation had changed. One must put oneself forward by opting to appear before a promotion board and be subjected to tough interviews about one's suitability, and by appearing before the board, candidates knew they stood some kind of chance – but if one failed to win promotion, then it was one's own fault! By submitting my name, I was announcing to the powers-that-be that I considered myself worthy of higher rank and capable of accepting more responsibility along with a supervisory role. All I had to do was prove it to that impressive gathering of very senior officers.

Now that the date had been announced, I became acutely aware that, somehow or other, I must endeavour to discover the sort of things I might be asked during the interview and was grateful for the long advance notice. It was then that I began to consider

the breadth of work and considerable responsibilities undertaken by someone like
Sergeant Blaketon as custodian of Ashfordly
section, and now by his replacement,
Sergeant Craddock. Not only did sectional
sergeants supervise the constables under
their command, they also dealt with the
administration systems necessary to run a
police station, prepared files for court and
made decisions about bail – they also pro-
secuted cases in the local magistrates'
courts and prepared inquests. Those duties
alone demanded a wide operational knowledge of criminal law, court procedures and
the laws of evidence. Now I knew why the
sergeant's office at Ashfordly Police Station
had shelves full of legal volumes like Stone's
Justices' Manual, Archbold's *Criminal Pleading, Evidence and Practice*, Paterson's *Licensing Acts*, Kenny's *Outline of Criminal Law*,
Oke's *Magisterial Formulist*, Wilkinson's
Road Traffic Offences, the *Manual of Guidance*
and others including the old faithful,
Moriarty's *Police Law* and volumes of the
magazine *Justice of the Peace* going back
decades.

Sergeants in the larger conurbations did
not necessarily prosecute in court but might
be called upon to do so; a newly promoted

sergeant usually worked in a town environment as part of a team, his duties comprising shift work under the supervision of an inspector. Following a period of this kind of work, a sergeant with potential for working on his own and making his own decisions, might be placed in sole charge of a small station like Ashfordly as a prelude to, and a means of training for, further promotion. In addition to their court work, sergeants were often called upon to act as friends, guides and counsellors to the constables under their command, particularly the younger ones, advising them on all manner of things like private domestic problems to their public role as police officers. They also required considerable administrative ability in order to manage a busy police office efficiently. This entailed everything from dealing with the station's financial budget to organizing the daily duties of everyone from the constables to the cleaner.

As the date of my interview drew nearer, therefore, I began to appreciate more fully the breadth of the duties and enormous responsibilities of what many called a humble sergeant. In truth, it was upon the shoulders of the sergeants that there rested much of the responsibility for managing the police service. I found myself observing Sergeant Craddock at work, and asking Oscar Blaketon for advice and guidance whenever the opportunity arose and, in addition, I began to study my law books, just as I had done prior to sitting my promotion examination; I wanted to be completely up-to-date in case the board asked me for comments about new legislation. They might question me on the problems of police procedures which could arise from the drink-driving laws, the new Criminal Justice Act or the abolition of felonies and misdeameanours in favour of the newly titled 'arrestable offences'. There were other similar possibilities, but the bobby on the beat cannot carry all those law books around with him before taking a particular course of action. There are times he must make an instant decision following which it might require lawyers and courts a period of many months' deliberation to determine whether or not he acted within the law – and it is the job of the sergeant to deal with that same incident, often on the spot and in the heat of the moment. Truthfully, I realized, a police sergeant requires a working knowledge and considerable expertise in a huge range of subjects and, I realized too, that a would-be sergeant must also possess that same knowledge in advance of promotion. It was vital that contenders had the ability to convince their superiors that they could fulfil the role of a sergeant in a calm, dignified and professional manner, especially while under pressure of any kind.

Perhaps fortuitously, it was while preparing myself for the interview that I received a request from the Brantsford Young Farmers' Club. They had been let down by a speaker and wondered if I could address them at short notice. After some discussion about a suitable subject, we produced a title – 'Farming and the Law'. The club had never previously been addressed by a police officer, but the secretary was aware that there was a wealth of law which could affect farms and farmers. He wanted information and advice from a practitioner rather than a solicitor. I stressed I had no knowledge of civil law, therefore my talk would have to concentrate on the criminal law so far as it affected the farming community, and I was told this was exactly what they required. As this seemed beyond the range of my normal duties, I felt

I ought to seek approval from higher authority and Sergeant Craddock had no objection to this so long as I stuck to the facts. And, he added, I could undertake the talk as part of my police duties – but, of course, I could not charge a fee.

And so it was that I found myself studying all the rules, regulations, laws and bylaws which affected farmers, and trying to find some way of presenting them in a simple but entertaining manner. I decided to make use of my own experiences and to reinforce them with examples of current law; I also discovered I could remember those laws after jotting down their titles and so it was that I gave my first legal lecture. I explained the law of treasure trove, should they find a hoard of gold or silver while ploughing, I touched upon matters like tractors leaving mud on the road, livestock straying on the highway, poaching, contagious diseases of animals such as swine fever, foot-and-mouth, fowl pest, glanders and farcy, and epizootic lymphangitis. I also touched upon the legal requirements when farm vehicles were used on public roads, the law on shotguns, rifles and air weapons with due emphasis on their use by young people on farm land. I covered cruelty to animals, the transit of animals, sheep worrying, dog collars, dog licences and exemptions, burial of animal carcasses, nuisances by animals and animal owners, lights on horsedrawn vehicles, the penalty for being drunk in charge of cattle, obstruction of public footpaths, theft of wild plants, the rules governing machines used for cutting hedges and verges, the movement of combine harvesters on the highway, and, of course, the effect of the all-important Musk Rats Order of 1932.

Delivering this talk without notes gave me a new confidence, especially when I could field a range of questions without reference to my copy of Moriarty's *Police Law* (which I had taken with me just in case I floundered), and I felt it helped to pave the way for my all-important date at Force headquarters. I believed I could address the promotion board without too much worry, although I would now have to increase my knowledge of the law to embrace a wider spectrum, like traffic law, betting, gaming and lotteries, drugs, or the effects of the Sexual Offences Act upon young people ... and if I jotted down the headings, I would remember the essence of each law. Then I wrote up my notes on *Farmers and the Law* and sent the article to a farming magazine which accepted it. Then I tried a similar tactic with the law on treasure trove, sending this to a treasure hunter's periodical, and a piece about poaching to a fishing journal ... and so, quite suddenly, I found myself absorbed in the odder aspects of criminal law and even sold articles to police and legal journals.

While this gave me a reason for studying all aspects of criminal law, including its history, it also increased my confidence because I knew I possessed a knowledge of law which should serve me well before the promotion board – and my writing provided a welcome and legitimate secondary income while not infringing Police Regulations. By chance, I had found a means of supplementing my income while remaining a police officer and this would benefit my family. I began to expand my writing by submitting articles on the countryside and the law to a variety of periodicals – I even had pieces published in *Punch*'s 'In the Country' column – and as a follow-up I found myself being asked to speak to other local organizations.

One morning, I received a letter which said, 'Dear Mr Rhea, By a grave misfortune,

229

I should have asked you to speak to our group on the 17th....' It was the 17th when her letter arrived and, while puzzling over this, I rang the lady to discover she'd forgotten to write to me earlier, but I had to decline, as I was on duty that evening – and she wanted a talk about the Dialect of the North Riding. Talks on police matters could be delivered during my duty time, but talks on other topics must be in my private time. In fact, I delivered only a handful of talks prior to my appointment with the promotion board although others followed and here are some notes on a few of the later and more memorable ones.

On one occasion, I drove across the Pennines into Lancashire, a return trip of 222 miles in total darkness, pouring rain and thick fog, to deliver a talk to a ladies' group. Before leaving I was ceremoniously presented with a small white envelope. Welcome petrol expenses, I felt! At home, I opened the envelope – it contained a book token for £1.

Another time, I drove about sixty miles to a venue to find a bridge, the only crossing place on a river and within the final mile or so, had been closed for repairs. This meant a detour of about twenty miles which, in turn, meant I arrived much later than the appointed time. I was then subjected to a public telling off by the chairlady and although I tried to explain I had not known, and could not have known, about the closed bridge so far from home, she simply said the ladies had been waiting in the cold hall and I should not have been late. Half past seven meant half past seven and not ten past eight! I didn't get a cup of tea or a bun either – not even a glass of water. Lady chairpersons can be very ferocious.

There was the time I drove through a ferocious blizzard with roads deep in snow and drifts blowing from the moors in order to fulfil a speaking engagement. I rang the secretary to ask if the meeting was going ahead in view of the atrocious weather, but she had gone out and her husband said she'd gone to the village hall. For that reason, I could only assume the meeting had not been cancelled and that I was required, and so off I went, armed with a snow shovel, wellies and warm clothing. When I arrived, I found two women huddled around a coke stove in the corner of the village hall – the secretary and her sister who was the caretaker – and so I delivered my talk to a captive audience of two.

One trick I quickly learned was never to arrive at the venue in time to sit through the meeting – having sat through a few very boring annual general meetings of the most obscure topics and associations, I began to ask the speaker-finders to suggest a time for me to arrive after the conclusion of the official part of meeting.

But it didn't always work. One speaker-finder rang to ask if I could talk to her members following the annual general meeting of the group, the Lingmell Society, and I agreed. I asked what time she expected the AGM to conclude, saying I would arrive in readiness for its conclusion whereupon she said she had no idea how long it would last and insisted I arrived at the very beginning of the event, so as not to interrupt the very important proceedings by arriving as they were in session. Anxious to please, I agreed, and found myself listening to a list of apologies for absence, the reading of the minutes of the last meeting, the reading of correspondence to the society, an account of the year's work, a wadge of reports by the secretary, treasurer and membership secretary; the appointment of a new president, chairwoman, secretary and treasurer, speeches by the outgoing officials and the incoming officials, the plans for the coming year with a proposed programme of outings, lots of thank-yous to lots of people and then the presentation of bouquets to various important persons, along with lots of polite applause in the right places. This went on and on and on – probably for a couple of hours or more, but when it was all over, I realized that after listening to their meeting, I had no idea of the function undertaken by the Lingmell Society. Whatever it was, it was important to its members but even today, I have no idea of its purpose or ideals. What on earth did the Lingmellers do when they were not holding meetings?

Perhaps the most curious was a talk to a Women's Institute high in the Yorkshire Dales, some seventy long and tortuous miles from my home in the North York Moors. I had been asked to attend a monthly meeting to speak about 'Dialects of the North Riding'; this was a light-hearted talk outlining the history of dialect but accompanied by humorous Yorkshire tales and a challenge to the ladies to tell me the meaning of some obscure dialect words and terms. I had delivered this talk many times and it was always popular and on this evening I found myself in the church hall of a small dales town with about 120 ladies from several local WIs. The president sat on the stage behind a table beautifully adorned with flowers and I was to join her; she would make the necessary introduction. I would deliver my talk standing up – this was another device which would maintain their interest and keep them awake. Vicars send their congregations to sleep during sermons because they cannot move around while isolated in the pulpit and so it is wise for a speaker to be able to move backwards and forwards across a stage or floor while speaking – which helps keep the audience alert and interested. And so I joined her on the stage in readiness for my address.

She rose to her feet and said, 'I would now like to introduce our speaker for this evening. He is Mr Charles Thompson who will talk to us about the Folklore of Yorkshire.' And to polite applause, she sat down.

I looked around for Mr Thompson, thinking I must have arrived on the wrong night, but as there was no sign of him, I realized she had made a big mistake but I decided I should not embarrass her. Fortunately, I have a good knowledge of the folklore of the Yorkshire Dales and North York Moors and so, on the spur of the moment, I delivered a talk about Yorkshire folklore.

There were a few questions afterwards which I was able to answer and finally, the president stood up and thanked me. 'Thank you very much for a fascinating talk, Mr Thompson. I am sure we will all travel around Yorkshire with a new interest in our surroundings and I know we are all fascinated by the moorland hobs, the Giant of Penhill and the Sunken Village of Semerwater, all so close at hand.' And then I went home, wondering what Mr Thompson would talk about when it was his turn to address them.

Talking to a wide variety of groups, especially the few I addressed prior to my promotion board, helped to improve my confidence before an audience and those early engagements contributed to my performance at the promotion board. On the day in question, I arrived at police headquarters in very good time and was able to scrounge a cup of coffee from an acquaintance before adjourning to the gents' toilet to give my boots a final polish, my uniform a final brush and my hair a last-minute comb. I sat my cap on my head in what I considered to be the correct angle, gripped my white gloves on my right hand (constables carried a pair of white cotton gloves in those days – I think it was in case they were faced with a sudden need or urge to perform traffic duty) and went along to the waiting-room. A sergeant of headquarters staff was waiting inside to greet me, as he had already greeted some candidates and, during the day, would greet more.

'PC Rhea, Aidensfield,' I announced.

He ticked me off the list which was pinned to a clipboard and said, 'Sit down, PC Rhea. I'll call you when you are required. It'll be about ten minutes.'

'Thanks, Sergeant,' and I plonked myself on one of the two chairs in the plain, unadorned room.

'When I call you,' he said, 'you will go through the door into the chief constable's office. The board will be sitting behind the chief's desk, facing the door as you enter. You march in briskly, come to attention before them and salute. Then remove your cap and sit on the chair, facing them, with your cap on your knee. And don't fidget with it. Sit there and answer the questions; don't just say 'Yes sir' and 'No sir' – talk about yourself, your work, your aims, expand things if you can, they like that. And relax as much as you can. I know it's not easy; it's a bit of an ordeal, but it's the same for everyone. It will take about twenty-five minutes or so, but no longer than half an hour. When you get the signal to leave, stand up, put your cap on, salute, do a smart about turn and march out. Right, any questions?'

'Will I be allowed to ask them questions?' I put to him.

'Yes, they'll give you that opportunity,' he assured me.

'Thanks. Is there someone in there now?' I asked.

'No, he's gone. They'll be writing up their notes about that interview and having a coffee break! You've come at a good time, they'll be more cheerful now they've had their coffee. Now, I'll go and wait outside the chief's office. And good luck.'

'Thanks, Sergeant.' Now I was nervous. Until this moment, I had felt quite calm and relaxed and, as I stood in that lonely, cheerless little room, my brain began to go over the topics I had studied. I found myself going over the provisions of the drink-driving laws, the new legislation about arrestable offences, the effect of the new

Criminal Justice Act, the proposals for new laws of gaming and for updating the law on larceny, burglary and associated crimes ... then there were drugs ... but from such a wealth of material, what were they likely to ask? I began to wonder if I really was ready for promotion...

'PC Rhea,' called the sergeant.

I went outside, my stomach now churning and my mouth feeling dry, and the sergeant said, 'This way.'

He led me along a wide and polished corridor lined with closed doors bearing labels like 'Deputy Chief Constable', 'Supt Admin', 'Accounts', 'Chief Constable's Secretary' and 'Typing Pool', and then we were in a small alcove containing two chairs. 'Sit down,' he said, and I did. He tapped on the big polished oak door which bore a sign saying 'Chief Constable' to which had been pinned another saying, 'Meeting in Progress'. A voice said, 'Come in', and the sergeant entered, closing the door behind himself. I was now alone and could hear my heart thumping. I gave my boots another quick polish on the legs of my trousers, adjusted my cap even though it was not necessary and swallowed to try and ease the dryness in my throat. Then the door opened and the sergeant called me.

'PC Rhea from Aidensfield, sir.'

I advanced with my heart pounding and he held open the big oak door and announced, 'Police Constable Rhea, Aidensfield, sir,' as I marched through.

He would close the door behind me, leaving me at the mercy of the row of uniformed officers. I stomped across the thick carpet and, as I did so, I could only think of a colleague who, in a similar situation, found himself marching across a polished floor towards his boss's desk. He came smartly to attention on the rug in front of the desk but the cleaner had polished the floor beneath it and as the constable's feet thudded to a halt, the rug slid away and carried him with it. He arrived very unceremoniously on the flat of his back beneath the knee-hole of the desk – but in this office, I was pleased to note, there was a fitted carpet. I thudded across it, arrived at the chair, flung up a salute and heard a voice say, 'Thank you, PC Rhea. Please sit down.' I sat on the chair, cap on my knees and my feet together, determined not to fidget with the cap or twiddle with my thumbs. As I settled down as best I could, I was aware of those figures in front of me, all bosses, all very senior police officers, all very powerful and all capable of deciding whether or not I was suited to further promotion. I waited. Nervous. Expectant. It was like a cross between waiting for the dentist to start drilling and the executioner testing his noose for comfort and size.

The chief constable began. 'Now, PC Rhea, how's life at Aidensfield?'

'Very good, sir,' I couldn't think of much else to say. 'It's most enjoyable, there's an interesting variety of work.'

'Not the busiest of beats, though, is it?' he continued, and I wondered if there was some hidden meaning in that question.

'There's enough to keep me occupied, sir,' I tried to justify my presence.

'I'm sure you are not bored, Rhea,' he said. 'But I see the crime figures for your beat are very low. Not much happens there, in other words, not many crimes for you to deal with or major problems to face?'

'I believe that a regular police presence, in uniform, is a good deterrent to crime, sir.' I felt I had to state my views. 'The crime rate is low because I make sure I am seen patrolling throughout my beat night and day. The uniform is always a deterrent and by that I mean it prevents minor crime too,

240

like acts of vandalism by young people, or petty thefts, car crime and that sort of thing.'

'That's a good theory, Rhea,' the deputy now entered the fray. 'But the alternative argument is that if there is a low crime rate in a particular area, then there is no need for a continuing police presence. We have to consider whether resident constables on the quieter rural beats can be justified, from a financial or manpower point of view. The Police Committee, and of course the Home Office, are always pressing us to be more cost effective and to cut unnecessary expenditure, and it does cost a considerable sum to maintain a constable on a rural beat, along with his house, transport and operating costs. So, if we were to dispense with Aidensfield beat, how do you think that would affect the crime rate, and what would be the reaction of the people?'

'Close it you mean, sir?' I must have sounded horrified. Close my beat! I didn't voice my concerns aloud, but could it mean my work at Aidensfield was valueless? That I was not doing a worthwhile or necessary job?

'It is no secret in our modern society that we must take a long, hard look at all our centres of operation, large and small, and decide whether or not some can be dispensed with, Rhea. If there is a low crime rate on a particular beat, the Home Office and our own Police Committee will question the need for a resident constable – it's based on a simple ratio which seeks to determine the cost effectiveness of maintaining a constable in an area where there is little or no serious crime.'

'But the whole point, sir, is that it is the presence of that constable which ensures a low crime rate,' I said, trying to state my opinion. 'If he was removed, then crime would rise – even if the police were not aware of that rise.'

'Not aware of it?' he frowned.

'If there was no constable patrolling the villages on a regular basis,' I said, 'the local people would not report crimes because there'd be no one to report them to. Crime would rise without the police being aware of it – it would be minor crime, I agree, but crime nonetheless. And that, in turn, would alienate the public. Lots of rural people regard the local constable as a kind of insurance policy – he's there if he's needed, and most hope they never need him. So I believe rural beats should be maintained, whatever the cost.'

'Victims of the kind you mention could telephone their nearest police station,' said the deputy. 'Either from home or from a kiosk.'

'Country people don't think like that, sir,' I told him. 'If a farmer or cottager has someone break a pane of glass in a greenhouse or steal a few eggs, the victims wouldn't ring up the police in Scarborough or Whitby or even Ashfordly. They'd mention it to the local constable next time they saw him, and he'd know if similar crimes had been committed locally ... you can't expect country people to think they're being a nuisance by formally reporting what they see as trivial matters. Stealing eggs is a crime in our books, sir, but in the countryside, it's little more than a nuisance. People will mention in passing to the constable in the hope he'll do something, to stop it happening again perhaps, but the last thing they want is any kind of official fuss. And lots of townspeople think likewise, and pensioners.

Next it was the turn of Superintendent Adamson, the commander of 'F' Division.

'To become a successful sergeant, PC Rhea, a constable needs a wealth of practical experience in a variety of different locations – town, country, motor patrol and so on. It is inevitable that he will have to draw on that experience sooner or later. Would you agree?'

'Yes, I would, sir.'

'But you do not have that kind of experience, Rhea.' He was not smiling as he launched that missive. 'I see from your record that you performed only two years on the beat at Strensford, and that was as a probationer constable, and then you were transferred to headquarters in an administrative capacity where you served for five years, and then you were posted to Aidensfield where you've been for, how long? Almost four years? That's eleven years' service, Rhea, going on twelve counting overlaps, but very little at what might be termed the sharp end of policing.'

'Much of the so-called sharp end, sir, is time spent dealing with things on a repetitive basis, drunks every Saturday night, regular fights outside dance halls and so on, cars broken into on the streets time after time, petty crimes by the score every day on housing estates. Lots of experience, certainly sir, but repetitive. You don't learn much from constant repetition. In my experience, limited though it might be, I have dealt with a variety of crimes, offences and incidents, ranging from fatal traffic accidents to rape, via arrests for larceny and lots of sudden deaths. Perhaps I have not experienced the volume of work at the so-called sharp end, but I have experienced a very wide variety. I consider that to be both important and valuable.'

'I see you have a commendation, Rhea, for detecting a crime?' put in Superintendent Sullivan of 'B' Division. 'You detected a raincoat theft two years after the crime had been committed? Tell us about it.'

'Well, sir,' I began. 'I went to a dance with my girlfriend, now my wife, and hung my brand new RAF-blue coloured raincoat in the cloakroom. When I returned to collect it, it had gone and a tatty old brown one, far smaller than mine, had been left in its place. I reported it to a constable on duty at the dance hall and then, two years later when I was on duty in Strensford Police Office, around 2 a.m. on New Year's morning, there was a vehicle crash outside the town, and the driver of one of the cars was brought into the station by the traffic department. I noticed he was wearing my coat, sir.'

'No, you misunderstand, Rhea. I am not concerned with a mix-up of your own raincoat, however important it was to you at the time. I am referring to this commendation, on your file, where you detected a crime which was two years old.'

'Yes, sir, that's it. That's what I'm saying, it was that case. It happened to be my own coat, sir. My coat had been stolen two years earlier, and the thief was wearing it when he was brought into the police station after that accident.'

'Your own coat?'

'Yes, sir.'

'And you recognized it after two years?'

'Yes, sir, it was quite distinctive. I had bought it just before leaving the RAF, sir, during my National Service, and had sewn my RAF number tag into the flap on the sleeve. When I asked the wearer to unbutton the flaps, sir, I saw he'd removed the number tags but tiny pieces of cotton had been left. He admitted stealing it and leaving his own in its place, even though it was a different size and colour.'

'So you got a commendation for detecting a crime in which you were the victim?'

'Yes, I thought it rather odd at the time, sir.'

'Well, this record doesn't inform us that the property was your own, but it was a piece of good work.'

'We recovered more coats as a result, sir,' I decided to add. 'My wife's cousin had two motor-cycling overcoats stolen a year before mine was taken, and a week after I recovered mine, his turned up in a cardboard box in his back garden.'

'So you solved three crimes, Rhea? All more than two years old?'

'Well, actually, sir, they'd been recorded as lost property, so we had a struggle finding the original reports...'

'Don't tell me any more, Rhea,' he laughed. 'And this wasn't the only crime you solved? I have a note in your file about some good work detecting a fraud, something to do with a building society pass book?'

I told him about that case. Whilst a young constable in Strensford I was told to make discreet enquiries in the town about the character of a man who had applied for a justices' licence in East Yorkshire. In his application, he had said he lived in Strensford. Off I went to the area in which he had quoted as his former address and I began to make discreet enquiries about him, visiting shops, pubs, bookmakers' shops, clubs and offices. No one knew him. At every place I asked about him and his character, he was unknown. Then the sergeant arrived and asked how I was progressing. When I said I'd found out absolutely nothing about the applicant, the sergeant said, 'Well, good, it means there's nothing known against him. Put that in your report, Rhea.' But I was not happy with that. In my view, if he'd lived in that locality, someone must have known him and so, almost in defiance of my sergeant, I intensified my enquiries and finally went to a house next door to the one he'd quoted as his former address. He was not known there either. And so, in one last attempt, I actually knocked on the door of the house he had given as his address. A young woman with a baby in her arms answered the door and when I said I was asking about the character of the gentleman in question, she burst into tears.

'That crook, that scheming b–d! He nicked my building society pass book, forged my signature and got away with more than eight hundred pounds!' As I was a mere probationary constable, the CID took the case from my hands but he was eventually charged with various offences of fraud – and he failed in his bid to get a justices' licence through which he was hoping to establish a restaurant.

And then, for good measure, I mentioned a case where a girl had been sexually assaulted by a youth and even though she gave the wrong time, and a misleading description, I managed to trace him. Then there was the case of a stolen chainsaw – which I detected.

'Thank you, PC Rhea,' said the super-intendent. 'You've made your point. It seems you do have some practical experience and a knack for detecting crime. I'm surprised you've never transferred to the CID.'

'The opportunity has not arisen,' I responded, and then it was the turn of my own superintendent, the officer in charge of 'D' Division.

'Promotion means a transfer, PC Rhea, and uprooting your family with schooling to consider and your wife to think about. For some wives, such a move can be very unsettling, it means leaving old friends and making new ones, children coping with a new school and so forth. Does that present any worries to you?'

'I have discussed it with my wife, sir,' I told him. 'Many times, in fact, and she will always support me in furthering my career. She has stressed that on many occasions, and we both feel the children might even benefit from the occasional change of school.'

There were a few more light-hearted questions, with nothing awkward about my views on new legislation and quite suddenly, it was all over. During my inquisition, I had lost my nervousness and quite enjoyed the banter, but whether or not I had succeeded in convincing those senior officers of my capability for higher rank remained to be seen. I rose from the chair in a bit of a daze, put on my cap, saluted and left the room, really wondering whether it had all been useful. Then I drove home and told Mary all about it, saying it would be a while before I knew the outcome.

She said, 'Well, I don't care whether you get promoted or not. I like it here, the children like the school and we've made a lot of nice friends. I think I'd like to stay in this area.

'Even if they close down Aidensfield beat?' I asked.

'You could always get another job,' she smiled, and I wasn't sure whether or not she was joking.

Chapter 8

Every day, printed circulars known as Crime Informations arrived by post at Ashfordly Police Station, and there were sufficient copies for distribution to all rural beats within Ashfordly Section, and for display on internal police noticeboards. These news-sheets comprised a digest of the main undetected crimes and other information of value to police officers throughout the North-East of England. They served the area east of the Pennines from the Scottish Border down to the Humber and included the Sheffield area which was then in the West Riding of Yorkshire. In most cases, the leaflets contained the names of persons suspected and wanted for arrest or interview about those crimes, and one of my daily tasks was to read them carefully.

In studying them, I was always surprised at the number of confidence tricksters who were sought, having stayed in boarding-houses or hotels and then left without paying the bill. Stolen cars, unrecovered for some weeks, also featured, as did photographs of antiques or valuable furniture stolen during housebreaking or burglary raids. These daily bulletins rarely contained details of very urgent or serious investigations like murders or rapes unless there was a particular reason for circulating some detail or other; rather, they contained more general information about lesser crimes which had remained undetected after a week or two. There were also details of a host of minor villains, often very mobile, who were sought for a variety of offences ranging from simple larceny to vandalism via fraud, motoring offences and even bigamy.

One of the most common features was the number of teenage girls who appeared under the heading 'Missing from Home'. Almost every day, several teenagers ran away from home within that region, usually girls but very occasionally boys; most were within the age group fifteen to seventeen and in many cases, the reason for the disappearance was given as 'Left home after a dispute with parents'. Teenagers who ran away from home after an argument fell into an awkward category so far as the police were concerned.

It was our policy not to search for adults who left unexpectedly – being adults, they were quite entitled to leave the family home if they wished and even if the relatives were upset, distressed and worried, it was not a matter for the police – unless there was reason to be concerned for their personal safety, or if they had either committed, or been the victim of, crime. In those latter instances, we would initiate a search and circulate details to neighbouring police areas. Likewise, if a young child vanished from home, there would always be a search, whatever the reason for his or her departure. But teenagers fell into that awkward category which was midway between children and adults. After all, a person can get married at the age of sixteen, but if we received a report that a teenager was missing, we would make very careful enquiries before deciding what action to take. There is little doubt that a lot of nubile girls ran away from home due to what one might call 'the wicked stepfather syndrome' – i.e. sexual acts or molestation by other members of her family, but it was extremely rare for such a case to reach court.

Families tended to keep such matters to themselves, not wishing the public or the police to know what went on behind the closed doors of the family home or bedrooms. Even though the police suspected that incest or other sexual offences were often reasons for teenage girls running away from home, it was very rare that such suspicions could be proved because the family closed ranks against any kind of investigation, and the girls in question would seldom, if ever, make a formal complaint to the authorities.

The police had the benefit of the Children and Young Persons Act of 1933 which stipulated the ages at which children could or could not do certain things, and for the 'Missing from Home' problem, it helped by clarifying the term 'child' and 'young person'. A child was defined as a person under the age of fourteen, while persons aged fourteen and up to seventeen were known as 'young persons'. For many legal purposes, an 'adult' was a person who had attained the age of seventeen, even though they could not buy liquor in the bar of a public house, could not take part in betting or gaming, could not vote and could not become a bus conductor. As if to confuse things, the Children Act of 1948, which was also then in force, defined a person under seventeen as a 'child', but for our practical police purposes a person who had attained the age of fourteen was a young person. If a youngster *under* fourteen ran away from home, therefore, we made every effort to trace them in the shortest possible time with as much publicity as reasonable in the circumstances, whereas if the runaway was fourteen or over, but under seventeen, then our reaction was less dramatic, albeit every case being dealt with on its merits.

There would be local enquiries while details of the youngster's absence, with a personal description and some details such as 'likes dancing' or 'is fond of horses and ponies' would be circulated in our Crime Informations if the absentee did not return within a day or two. More often than not it was a case of maintaining a watching brief in case the missing youngster was sleeping rough or hanging around bus stations, cafés and such places. In almost every case of a teenager running away from home in my part of the world, they returned within a few days and we crossed them off our 'Missing from Home' lists, seldom enquiring the reason for their departure. After all, purely domestic issues and family rows were not usually a matter for the police.

When fourteen-year-old Emily Jordan disappeared, therefore, I found myself experiencing mixed reactions. Her parents were very decent people; she had a nice sister and brother, both younger than she; she seemed happy at school and enjoyed a cheerful circle of friends both in Aidensfield where she lived and Ashfordly where she attended a secondary modern school. There seemed to be no logical reason why she should run away and that meant the police had to examine the likelihood that something unexpected had happened to her. An accident perhaps? Abduction even? Had she run off with a boyfriend? That was not uncommon. Girls would leave home with boyfriends, hoping for a blissful, romantic and very wonderful new life in some town like London or Newcastle ... in such cases, the reality quickly sent them scurrying back home.

I sat at the kitchen table of the Jordans' semi-detached home on Sycamore Lane, Aidensfield, with my notebook open and pen poised as I tried to elicit as much information as possible from her distraught parents. Her father, Jim, was manager of Ashfordly Co-Op while her mum, Shirley, had a part-time job in a souvenir shop in

Strensford. It was late – half-past midnight in fact, and both were in a miserable state. They had sent their other children to their rooms while we talked but we knew they would not go to sleep. Mrs Jordan had produced mugs of tea and biscuits for us and, having first listened to their account, I now had to try and establish some kind of chronological sequence of events prior to Emily's disappearance with, if possible, some hint of a reason for her absence. I checked the notes I had already made.

'So, Jim and Shirley, you say Emily was here this morning at eleven. You'd already had your own breakfasts, and so had Jane and Terence, but Emily was late up.'

'We'd planned to go to Hornsea for the day,' Jim reminded me. 'A family outing, something we like to do on Sundays, but Emily said she didn't want to go because she'd promised her friend, Sally, she'd see her. They were talking of going for a bike ride.'

'Sally Upton?' I checked my notes.

'Yes, Ashdale Farm. They've been good friends for years, but Sally has no idea where Emily's gone. I rang her but she said she hadn't agreed to spend today with Emily and knew nothing of a supposed bike ride.'

'So Emily lied to you?' I stated the obvious.

'It looks like it,' and Shirley began to weep once more. 'I never thought she'd ever be deceitful, Mr Rhea, not Emily. She's always been so open and trustworthy, always, ever since she was little. And she lied to Sally as well ... I'm sure Sally is telling the truth when she says she has no idea where Emily has gone.'

'It is odd, I must admit. Now, you left home just before eleven-thirty?'

'Yes, I asked her again if she'd like to come with us, but she was adamant she didn't want to, saying Sally would be here soon and they'd arranged to take a flask, and some sandwiches to eat on their ride. We left her eating her breakfast, Mr Rhea, and she said she'd make her own sandwiches. We got home about half past five this evening and she wasn't here; the key was under the mat – we always do that when we're out and at first we thought nothing of it. We knew if she'd gone out with Sally, she might be at Sally's house. There was no note to say where she'd gone, and her bed was made – she'd even washed her breakfast pots.'

'So what time did you contact Sally?'

'We waited until ten o'clock, that's about

half an hour after Emily's normal bedtime and it was dark by then, and that's when I rang Dan Upton to see if Emily was at his house. But she wasn't, he'd not seen her and Sally had been at home all day; they'd had her grandparents over from Thirsk. Dan asked Sally if she'd promised to go on a bike ride with Emily and she said she hadn't. That's when we decided to ring you. I'm sorry to drag you out so late but we are desperately worried, Mr Rhea.'

'And rightly so,' I tried to reassure them. 'I don't mind being called out, this is no frivolous matter. So has she taken anything with her? Clothes? Toiletries? Suitcase or holdall? School things?'

'Oh dear, I don't know,' Shirley said, sniffing away her tears. 'Shall I go and have a look?'

'Mind if I come?' I asked.

'No, not at all, you know what you're looking for, Mr Rhea.'

It was clear from Emily's bedroom that she had not taken any extra clothes, nor she had taken any of her toiletries such as her own soap and toothbrush. In my mind, this added an ominous tone to her disappearance – if she'd run off with a boyfriend or in fit of pique over some domestic drama, she'd have taken something with her – but nothing was missing from her room. And her room was very tidy indeed; the house had been locked in the family's normal manner so there was no indication she'd been attacked.

'What about her bike?' I asked Jim when I went back downstairs.

'It's not here,' he told me. 'That was the first thing I checked, and naturally I thought she was with Sally, on a bike ride somewhere. I'll show you where it's kept.'

This time, Jim took me outside to a shed at the rear of the house, and when he opened it, it contained two other bikes belonging to Terence and Jane, but Emily's was missing.

'Does she often ride it?' I asked.

'Quite often,' he nodded. 'She uses it when she goes up to Ashdale Farm to see Sally, and sometimes she goes off for short rides on her own, up and down the village and so on, so yes, she uses it quite a lot.'

I then obtained a description of the missing girl. She was about five feet two inches tall with an average build, dark, shoulder-length hair and brown eyes. She had a few freckles on her face which she tried to conceal with make-up, and was wearing a blue woollen jumper, a short white skirt and calf-length white leather boots. As her father had been unable to afford a new bike, her cycle had been assembled by him from bits and pieces he'd acquired second-hand, and it was a lady's style with a green frame, but with dropped handbars to give it a sporty appearance.

'Before I circulate a description of her,' I told them. 'I must ask if there has been a family row of some kind, a dispute, something that would cause her to run away. Boyfriend trouble even? And then I must search the house. Cases have occurred of youngsters getting locked in wardrobes or hiding in the attic or outbuildings, even while a search is being made.'

'Is that really necessary?' asked Shirley, slightly haughtily. 'Searching the house, I mean?'

'I'm afraid so,' I told her, not adding that it was also known for parents or other family members or friends to have killed children and hidden their bodies until the fuss had died away.

'Well, I hope the house is clean where you search, and heaven knows what you'll find under the childrens' beds, and as for our wardrobes...'

'I'm not here to look at clothes and worry about a bit of dust.' I tried to ease her mind a little. 'All I want to do is to find Emily.'

'Mr Rhea knows what he is doing, Shirley,' said Jim quietly.

'Yes, I know, I'm sorry, it's all so up-setting...' and she burst into tears and fled into the lounge. Jim assured me there had been no domestic row with Emily, adding that her decision to forego the family outing had not caused problems. They appreciated she was growing up quickly and no longer wanted to do childish things like having days at the seaside with her parents.

'And there's no boyfriend trouble, Mr Rhea,' Jim assured me. 'She's never been a problem. She's a lovely girl ... this is totally out of character, we've barely had a cross word with her, apart from the usual things like getting up late and not doing her home-work ... and she went through a phase of wanting a bedroom of her own with a radio in it instead of sharing with Jane. Then she wanted a pony and got upset when I wouldn't allow it, well I couldn't, could I? Not with only a patch of lawn to keep it on! She likes animals you see, and we let her keep rabbits and guinea pigs when she was younger, and a cat. But as for running away, this is not Emily, definitely not.' I could see he was getting emotional now. I began to wonder if he was, however unwittingly, the cause of her disappearance. Was he very strict with her? 'Look, I'd better show you round, Mr Rhea.'

Upstairs, I went into the loft, searched beneath all the beds and in all the wardrobes, the airing cupboard and a linen chest, and downstairs went behind the settee and easy chairs, behind the curtains, into the pantry and all the outbuildings.

I made sure I checked the garden shed and the outside toilet, and even the garden for signs of recent soil movements. But there was no sign of Emily.

'I'm sorry about that, Shirley,' I apologized. 'But we have to check thoroughly before we formally record her as missing. So I believe something has happened and the first thing is to alert our officers. Can I use your phone?'

'Yes, of course.'

I chose to do this rather than use the official radio because it meant the family could hear what steps I was taking to find Emily. I rang Ashfordly Police Station and Phil Bellamy answered; he was working a night shift.

'Phil,' I said, 'it's Nick Rhea. I'm ringing from the home of Mr and Mrs Jordan in Aidensfield,' and I provided their address and telephone number. I explained about Emily's mysterious disappearance and provided him with a description of her and her bike. 'Can you check all the hospitals and the ambulance service to see if there is any report of an accident involving her or her bicycle? I don't suppose she's ridden far, but if she's got a puncture or a broken chain or something, then she might have been marooned somewhere. Contact all police stations within a forty-mile radius, Phil, to see if they've any reports of such an incident, and circulate the girl as Missing From Home. I'm satisfied there has been no domestic dispute and I don't think a boyfriend is involved. She hasn't taken any clothes or belongings with her, so we need to treat this with some urgency.'

'If she had fallen off her bike,' whispered Shirley in my ear, 'she'd have telephoned or got a message to us somehow.'

'Not if she's unconscious,' I heard myself say. 'And would she have any means of identification on her?'

'Oh, no, I doubt it...'

I must admit that all kinds of possible

scenarios flashed through my mind as I was making that call, and I felt the most logical explanation was that Emily had had some kind of mishap involving her bicycle. That raised a distinct likelihood that she'd been injured or rendered unconscious. And if she had no means of identification, then whoever was caring for her now would have no idea who she was or where she lived. She could be lying in some hospital bed with concussion, or worse, lying in a ditch hidden from passers by. Phil promised to do all he could to trace her.

Although it was now almost one o'clock, I had a chat with the wideawake Terence and Jane to see if they could provide me with any clues about the reason for her absence, but they could not. They added that Emily did not confide in them – 'We're much too young for her!' said Jane, aged nine, a statement with which eleven-year-old Terence agreed. Shirley confirmed that Emily was very secretive, often spending time alone in her room with a book or listening to the radio, and not sharing her day's joys and disappointments with her brother and sister, or her parents, but apart from that characteristic, she was a lovely girl with no problems and she was a credit to her family.

Having squeezed as much information as possible from the Jordans and having also acquired a photograph of Emily for use if necessary, I left them with a request that if they heard from her, they should inform me as soon as possible, whatever the time of night. I assured them that Phil Bellamy would circulate her details to every police station and hospital within miles, and that all our night patrols would keep an eye open for her. I assured them I would examine all the ditches and roadside verges in the locality before I went home, while Jim said he would visit all her known friends and acquaintances just in case she had been in contact with any of them. I suggested that Shirley remain at home, near the telephone, in case a call came from Emily or anyone else, and she said she would do that.

'If she does come home,' I said to Shirley, 'don't rant and rave at her, cuddle her, make her welcome ... she might have had a very tough time.'

'I'll do my best,' she assured me, adding, 'it's been tough for me too.'

'But you're a parent, you have to be tough,' I smiled, adding after a moment, 'I know you'll do well.'

'You really think she'll come home?' she

put to me.

'Yes I do, but sadly, I don't know when.' I had to be honest. 'Why not go to bed? You'll need the rest and you'll hear the phone.'

'I couldn't, not with Jim out looking. But thank you for what you've done so far.'

'I've not done anything yet,' I said. 'But I'm going to search the village before I turn in. Come along, Jim, you can help me. We've a lot to do.'

I suggested that Jim visit all her friends from school, including those youngsters in Aidensfield and nearby who attended other schools. Emily had a wide circle of friends from her primary-school days when they'd visited each other's homes, attended parties and even slept over as youngsters do.

'Sure. I'll visit every house I can remember,' he said. 'And I'll keep an eye open for her bike.'

'I'll check all the road verges in and around the village,' I assured him. 'There are some accident black spots, where a bike might run away if the brakes failed and where someone could be lying injured, well away from the eyes of passersby. I want to tour all my patch – Aidensfield first, then Elsinby, Briggsby and so on, and any other place she might have ridden to.

'Thanks,' he said. 'It's nice to know we're getting help with this. I'm sorry it's happened so late at night.'

'Forget it, it's my job,' I told him. 'Now, we need to rendezvous somewhere, to check each other's results.'

'If I go home I'll not go to bed, Mr Rhea, and neither will Shirley, not until Emily's found. It might be easier if you check at our house every hour or so, until we feel we've done all we can. Shirley will take any messages.'

'I'll do that, but first I'll call at my own house to tell my wife what's going on, otherwise she'll think I've had an accident or something!'

And so, as Jim Jordan went off in his car to begin his own search, I decided to check all the known hills, corners and accident black spots on my patch, looking into the woods and moorland which bordered the steep and twisting lanes just in case the unfortunate girl's brakes had failed and she'd careered wildly off the highway and crashed. Or of course she might have been the subject of a hit-and-run driver, and be lying injured somewhere. Time was moving rapidly and finding her was a forlorn hope in the darkness of the vast empty landscape, but a search must be made. When I popped home to tell Mary what was happening, she was still up, waiting for some news from me, so I suggested she go to bed. She smiled and said she would, even if she'd not be able to sleep. As she was preparing for bed, I rang Ashfordly Police Station from my office telephone and Sergeant Craddock answered.

'Ah, PC Rhea, glad you've made contact. Any news?'

He listened carefully as I outlined my actions to date, and the part now being played by her father, and then he said, 'PC Bellamy had the sense to alert me to this, we must take it seriously. You ought to know that we've checked all the local hospitals and ambulance services and they've no reports of her being involved in an accident, and we've nothing back from neighbouring police stations either. Look, Bellamy and I will come to Aidensfield and help in your search, but have we reached the point where we need to arrange a formal search party? Police dogs? Searchlights? That sort of thing?'

'It's difficult to say, Sergeant,' I had to admit. 'Teenage girls do stay out late, I'm sure you know that, and it's only a few hours since I was informed of her absence. She might be visiting a friend and have forgotten what time it is. Youngsters do that – I know I did! My mother used to get very, very cross when I rolled up at two in the morning to say I'd just been chatting with friends and had forgotten the time. Time can run away with you. Besides, her bike's not been found abandoned anywhere, she's not taken any clothes or toiletries with her, so I tend to believe she is still somewhere nearby. I'm veering towards the idea she might have had a cycling accident and be lying badly injured somewhere.'

'That sounds logical to me. We'll come anyway and we'll help you to search locally before we bring in the heavy guns. So where shall we meet?'

'I'm going to head towards Briggsby first,' I told him. 'I want to search both sides of the road where it descends through Hollybush Wood; there's some tricky corners there and I've known very experienced cyclists come to grief, especially when gravel collects on the bends after heavy rain.'

'We'll see you there. We'll look for your van.'

'I doubt she'll have gone much further in that direction,' I said.

'Don't worry, we'll check likely places along the roadside verges between Ashfordly and there as we come towards you.'

I told Mary about that arrangement, and the arrangement I'd made with Jim Jordan, then left to begin what might become a long night's work.

In heading for Hollybush Wood, I stopped several times *en route* so that I could check various bends and dips, but found no sign of anyone crashing through hedges, running across verges or being involved in an accident. I parked on a wide verge at the summit and left the headlights blazing to provide more light, and then decided to walk down one side of the hill and return up the other, checking every inch of the way. It was then that Sergeant Craddock and Phil Bellamy arrived. After a brief discussion, Craddock asked for suggestions for places that could be searched by him and Bellamy, and I suggested Elsinby Hollows. He and Phil would go on ahead and search the steep hills around that area. I told them I'd arranged to meet up with Jim Jordan at his home for regular rendezvous and they said they'd attend, too. And so we got some kind of search underway, but my examination of the long road through Hollybush Wood produced nothing.

Time had flown and already it was time for my rendezvous with Jim Jordan. I regained my van, turned it around in a gateway and headed across the heights back to Aidensfield. As I did so, I saw another vehicle heading towards me, climbing the steep hill out of the village and I decided to stop it and ask the driver if he'd seen a girl or a cycle or both. I knew it wasn't Craddock – he was some two miles away in the opposite direction, but the engine noise told me it was a small vehicle, a private car perhaps. I switched on my blue light, parked the van at the road side and climbed out armed with a handtorch which I waved up and down as an order for the driver to halt. In the glare of its headlights, it was difficult to see clearly but the driver had the courtesy to lower the window as I approached.

It was Beatrice Cooper, the vet from Ashfordly, and she looked as if she'd been helping an elephant give birth or something similar. She was dirty and bloodstained and very unkempt.

'Oh, hello, Beatrice,' I said, letting her see my face and uniform. 'You're out late. Been to a party, have you?'

'Some party! Working late is one of the

hazards of the profession, Nick, like your job,' she chuckled. She was a plump, jolly woman in her thirties. 'Is this a breath test or something?'

'No, nothing like that,' I told her. 'I'm looking for a girl who's missing from home. I saw the car coming and wanted to ask the driver if he or she had seen anything of her. So here you are. She went off on her bike earlier today and hasn't come home.'

'Who is it?' she frowned.

'Emily Jordan,' I said. 'She's fourteen. I'm not sure if you know the family...'

'Yes, of course I do. Do you mean there's a search party out for Emily?'

'In a small way, yes,' I said, and explained the story.

Beatrice got out of her car as I was telling the tale and sighed, her voice showing signs of severe tiredness. 'Nick, you're not going to like this.'

'Like what?' I asked, as we stood on that hilltop with our headlights blazing and engines ticking over in the darkness.

'She's at Beckside Farm, in Maddleskirk. Alec Hepburn's place.'

'You're joking!'

'No, I'm not. She's there now, if she hasn't already left to go home.'

'But is she hurt? Did she have an accident or something?'

'Nothing like that, Nick. Look, I had no idea she might cause some kind of international incident. She said her parents knew where she was and told us she had a key to get in. I don't think she realized it was so late.'

'They're worried sick about her, Beatrice; they had no idea where she was and they've called us out. We're searching for her, thinking she must have had an accident, or been kidnapped, or worse.'

'Oh, crumbs, you can't rely on kids, can you!'

'So what's she doing at Beckside? And why is she out until this hour?'

'Alec'll probably give her a lift home in his Landrover. She's safe enough,' Beatrice said, rubbing her eyes and yawning.

'Come along, Beatrice! What's the story?'

'She's horse mad – maybe you didn't know that – and she's made pals with Alec's daughter, Sarah. Emily's folks won't let her have a pony, let alone a horse, so you can imagine how she worships those at Beckside.'

'They can't let her have one, Beatrice, not in a semi with a pocket-sized back garden!'

I laughed.

'Right, I know that, but to fulfil her horsy dreams, she's been going to visit Sarah at Beckside where they have lots of them. I've no idea whether she told her parents about this friendship – the Hepburns are nice people – but she's a very secretive girl, Nick. I wouldn't be surprised if her parents knew nothing of it.'

'I don't think they did. And tonight?' I asked.

'One of their mares was due to give birth and it turned out to be a very difficult one. That's what I've been doing, attending the birth. It took a long time; a long, long time in fact. I've been there ages, hours and hours. Emily was there throughout, helping, and did a really good job. I think she has the makings of a vet, I found her very capable and sensible, but she wouldn't go home until she knew the foal was all right. She told us her folks knew where she was... Oh dear, this doesn't sound very convincing, does it?'

'It does!' I assured her. 'It sounds very convincing indeed, so far as a teenager is concerned. So where is Emily now?'

'She was going to leave soon after me, but she wanted to see the foal settled down for the night with its mum.'

'Right, I'll go straight to the Jordans now, and give them the good news.'

'They won't be too hard on her, will they? She really was a great help, Nick. You could always blame me!'

'Thanks, Beatrice, I'll tell them. And you've just saved the constabulary a lot of expense and boot leather! And how is the new arrival?'

'Mother and daughter are both as well as can be expected,' she smiled, returning to her car. 'And I'm going home for a hot bath, a nice glass of brandy and then a nice long sleep – unless some other animal needs my attention before dawn!'

I radioed Sergeant Craddock and Bellamy and gave them the news, then said I was going immediately to the Jordans' home.

I arrived as Jim was trudging up his front garden path, looking distraught and tired after the first leg of his search.

'Anything?' he asked, without much hope in his voice.

'Yes,' I said. 'She's safe and sound ... she's been helping a mare give birth to a foal ... ah, this will be her.'

'You mean it?' and his face brightened.

'Yes,' and I began to explain. As we talked,

we heard the distinctive sound of a Land-rover chugging towards the house and soon the lights appeared. I waited long enough to see the pale face of Emily in the passenger seat, then said, 'She's all yours now, Jim. Don't be too hard on her; she did a good job tonight and deserves a lot of praise. Beatrice Cooper thinks she's got the making of a vet.'

And I decided to leave before I became embroiled in their private solution to this domestic drama.

Another youngster who created a flutter of alarm was ten-year-old Craig Fielding, an only child who lived with his parents in a house close to the shop in Aidensfield. A pupil at the village primary school, he was very sensitive and something of a loner who seemed to prefer the companionship of his black-and-white springer spaniel to that of other children. Ever since he was six or seven years old, Craig and his dog, called Glyn, could often be seen going on long walks around the village, venturing along the river-side or into the woodlands and even on to the loftier heights of the moors.

During his exploration of the district, Craig had gradually developed an interest in wild birds. His parents had bought him a reference book containing coloured pictures of British birds and so he would disappear for extended periods, sometimes with a picnic for himself and Glyn, to record all the species he noticed around him. An aunt had bought him a pair of binoculars for a birthday present and so he was able to pursue his bird-watching hobby with skill and enthusiasm. In his own quiet way, Craig had become quite an expert on the bird life of Aidensfield and district.

Then one day, Craig disappeared. The alarm was raised by the headmistress, Josephine Preston, herself a nature lover and expert on butterflies. Shortly after assembly that Wednesday morning, she rang Craig's mother, but unfortunately Mrs Fielding had already gone out shopping and Mr Fielding was at work, and so the message failed to reach them. Throughout the morning, Miss Preston had persistently rung the Fieldings' but there was no reply; Mr Fielding was a van driver and Miss Preston's enquiries from neighbours showed he was somewhere in Northumberland, out of contact.

Growing increasingly worried by the boy's non-appearance at school, and unable to contact his parents, Josephine rang me. By this stage it was the middle of the morning so I went immediately to the school. She took me into her tiny office and I could see the concern on her face; a fair-haired, petite young woman in her early thirties, she was highly attractive and well liked by everyone, including the pupils.

After listening to her version of events, I suggested, 'Perhaps he's gone off with his mother on some important and urgent matter? Maybe they left home early, too early to inform you perhaps?'

'That's what I thought, Nick,' she sighed. 'But I've managed to talk to Mrs Brownlow, their neighbour, and she saw Craig leave home for school as usual, just after half past eight. Mrs Fielding left home shortly after nine, so I must have just missed her. It seems she always goes to Ashfordly on a Wednesday morning, to catch the shops before they close for half-day. She has her own car and usually meets a friend in town where they have lunch, and she returns in time for Craig going home.'

'And Craig's dad?'

'He's up in Northumberland somewhere, delivering to hotels, but I can't get hold of him and his firm has tried; they've left messages at places he's expected to visit but so far he's not called me.'

'Normally, if a child is absent, you'd expect a note or phone call?'

'Yes, we insist on the correct procedures, just in case some children play truant, so when there was no message from Craig's parents, I rang them at the first opportunity – but I've got nowhere, Nick.'

'Right, I'll go to the house and have a snoop around, just to see if he's hiding there for any reason and I'll ask around the village to see if he's been seen anywhere away from his normal route. You keep trying to ring his parents as well and do whatever your rules and regulations stipulate. In view of the fact he's been missing for more than three hours and he's only ten, I think we'd better set all the formal procedures in motion. I'll keep in touch with you during the day – let's hope he turns up before night! But what's your opinion on this? Is he playing truant? Has he had problems at school?'

'He's not had problems, Nick. He's a quiet lad who seems to like his own company, but he's not been bullied or teased, and he's not been in trouble from any of the staff. If he is playing truant, there must be a reason I don't know about. It does look like truant, doesn't it?'

'Up to a point.' I had to admit, I was not

fully convinced. 'Setting off for school and not arriving is the sort of thing a truant would do, but there's usually a reason for that, something associated with the school, bullying, teasing, not coping with lessons and so on. I can't see why he'd bunk off school without a reason.'

'That's what bothers me,' she admitted.

I obtained a brief description from Josephine – Craig would probably be wearing school uniform (a blue blazer and grey shorts) but before contacting Sergeant Craddock at Ashfordly Police Station, I decided to establish, in my own mind, that Craig really was absent from his usual haunts. When I arrived at his home, the door was locked and it was clear his parents were still out. I went to see Mrs Brownlow, the neighbour and she confirmed Josephine Preston's account – Craig had definitely left for school at half-past eight this morning, without his dog, and she expected Mrs Fielding to return from Ashfordly about 2.30. She'd taken the spaniel with her in the car.

I considered asking Ashfordly Police to keep a look-out for her – there weren't that many eating places in the town – but now realized I must formalize things by informing Sergeant Craddock. Any report of a missing child must be taken very seriously. As I walked through the village, I asked everyone I met if they'd seen Craig this morning, and none had: it seemed almost certain he had not returned home or ventured through the village. I left messages at the shop, the post office and the pub with the idea of circulating Craig's absence to as many people as possible within Aidensfield, and from my own office, I rang Ashfordly Police. Alf Ventress answered. When I explained things, he said he knew Mrs Fielding by sight and would visit likely eating places in Ashfordly in the hoping of finding her while Sergeant Craddock decided he would circulate details of the missing boy.

'We need to arrange a search party, PC Rhea,' he added. 'You get something to eat straightaway while I'm driving out to join you; it could be a very long day and right. I'll bring PCs Ventress and Bellamy and we'll conduct a preliminary search of all likely places. And if we don't find him, we'll have to consider bringing in police dogs, more volunteers, specials and so on, to expand the search area. And if PC Ventress does locate Mrs Fielding, I'll ask her to get in touch with you immediately.'

As I ate a hurried early lunch, Monica Fielding rang me from a kiosk in Ashfordly, her voice revealing her concern. Trying not to sound alarmist, I explained the situation and she confirmed Craig had gone to school as usual this morning with no signs of reluctance, and he had taken a small satchel containing a sandwich, slice of fruit cake, an apple, and a bar of chocolate, along with a bottle of squash to drink. Children were taking pack-ups to school because of problems with the cooker – school meals were not available that week. She said she was returning to Aidensfield straight away and would come directly to the police house; she confirmed that the spaniel, Glyn, was with her in the car. If Craig had made deliberate plans to miss school, his arrangements had not included his dog.

By the time I had finished lunch, Sergeant Craddock and his team had arrived at my police house, and so had Mrs Fielding. As Mary produced cups of coffee for us, we adjourned to the office to study a large-scale map of Aidensfield in an effort to determine where the boy might have gone. In doing so, we also discussed the best means of co-ordinating our search, bearing in mind the extent and ruggedness of parts of the territory. As we discussed our ideas, we included Mrs Fielding because she showed commendable calmness and common sense, not panicking or becoming hysterical and over-demanding as some mothers might have done in the circumstances. Gently, she reminded us that Craig knew the district intimately, he and his dog regularly explored the whole area during his bird-watching expeditions and she'd never had any real concerns about his safety. He was very sensible.

'Are you saying he might have gone bird-watching?' Craddock frowned at her.

'I don't think he would play truant just to watch the birds,' she told us. 'He does have a sense of responsibility. I can't honestly see him playing truant due to some trouble at school; there's never been any sign of that and he's very happy there. But he is extremely keen on bird-watching and he's quite accustomed to going off with only his dog for company.'

'So do you think he would take a day off school, without permission, just to go bird-watching?' asked Craddock.

'I'd be very surprised if he did,' admitted Mrs Fielding. 'But it's the only likely answer, isn't it?'

284

'I didn't find anyone who saw him in the village after school time started,' I told them. 'If he has gone off on his own, he's chosen his destination quite carefully, well away from public places. And I didn't find evidence of anyone hanging around the village, so I don't think he's been joined by anyone.'

'You don't think he's been kidnapped, do you?' asked Mrs Fielding.

'I've absolutely no reason to think that,' I tried to reassure her. 'But it's something we can't ignore. I'm pretty sure he's involved in some very important but very personal enterprise today – his packed lunch suggests that. Has he mentioned rare birds in the area? Or some unusual sightings, that sort of thing?'

'No,' she shook her head. 'He's always talking about the birds he's seen on his outings, but I don't think he's noticed anything rare or special. His dad and I try to show an interest in his hobby and he does talk to us about it. If there was something rare in the area, I think he'd have told us.'

'Right,' said Sergeant Craddock, taking command of the situation. 'I think we must search the village and its surrounds thoroughly concentrating on places a young bird-watcher might go. Woods, the river-banks, the open moors, those sort of places. And Mrs Fielding? I think you should go home and be close to the telephone – and you might keep trying to locate your husband and get a message to him. If he does contact you, ask if he has any idea where Craig might have gone.

'Yes, yes, of course. I'll do that but I would like to do something positive.'

'We'll divide to make our search,' Craddock told her. 'There's four of us which means we can search four areas at one time. You'd be much more useful to us if you remained near the telephone, in case we need to contact you via our office in Ashfordly or if someone else needs to call you about Craig. And you would be able to consider other places Craig might have gone to.'

'Yes, I think I understand.' She was now showing signs of worry as the full significance of the occasion began to make its impact.

'I ought to search the house and out-buildings,' I put to Craddock.

'Yes, you go home with Mrs Fielding, PC Rhea, and conduct that search while I brief PCs Ventress and Bellamy. I will allocate the western banks of the river to you, PC Rhea, along with the woods which border them,' and he showed me the relevant place on the map.

'Fine, I know the area,' I assured him.

'Take your van as close as possible to the search scene and remain in radio contact if you possibly can. We will do the same. Rendezvous back here at the police house at, say, four o'clock?'

'Right, Sergeant,' I said. 'And on my way to the river-side, I'll tell the headmistress what we're doing.'

'Good. Well, off we go.'

In her own car, with the spaniel still in the rear, Mrs Fielding followed me to her home and together we made a careful search of the entire property, including the attic, toilets, wardrobes, outbuildings and garden sheds but there was no sign of Craig. He'd not returned home since this morning and now Mrs Fielding was showing more signs of distress. Glyn came to fuss over her, and then I had an idea.

'Mrs Fielding, why don't I take Glyn with me? He might help in my search.'

'Yes, do that, Mr Rhea. He always went with Craig and he'll know Craig's favourite places. He's very obedient; you can let him off the lead if you want.'

I told her not to be afraid of ringing my wife, Mary, or the police station at Ashfordly if she wanted more information or advice, or of course, if Craig returned home. After reassuring her that everyone was doing their best to find Craig, I popped the dog, complete with lead, into the rear of my van and drove towards the river. I could park near the bridge at the bottom of the village and walk along the riverbank for almost two miles, checking the bordering woodland, the river itself and several fields *en route*, including the cricket field.

Glyn was easy to control and, as Mrs Fielding had said, when I let him off the lead and tested him with a few commands, he obeyed instantly. I felt confident enough to let him find his own way ahead of me, snuffling in the undergrowth and ferreting among the grass and earth in the hope he'd come across his young master's scent. Together we began our search with me calling him to heel from time to time and asking him to search difficult areas – when I called 'Seek' he would rush into the area, sniffing and scenting the air, sometimes to be rewarded by startling a pheasant or blackbird and sometimes disturbing a snoozing rabbit or vole. It was a long semi-circular walk along the river-bank, the sort of walk one would normally undertake for pleasure, but I had no time to admire the surrounds or savour the atmosphere as I concentrated upon places likely to hide a small boy or even places in the river into which a small boy might fall. I realized I had forgotten to ask if Craig could swim...

There is not the space to dwell upon the delights to be found during an extended river-side walk but eventually I arrived at the southern tip of the large oval field which was used both by a contented herd of dairy cows and by Aidensfield cricket team. A pair of anglers was sitting near the edge of the river beneath the banks of the field, their concentration fully upon their lines and spinners and not upon people like me who happened to walk past. At this point, the banks were some six or eight feet high and very sandy, and so the fishermen would be invisible from most of the field, but not from me as I walked around the rim. I stopped and addressed them; they were a couple of men from Elsinby, I noted. I'd often seen them in the Hopbind Inn, although I did not know their names. Each would be in his mid-thirties, I estimated, but they had all the gear of a pair of dedicated fishermen.

'I'm searching for a missing boy,' I began, and followed with a description of Craig, explaining how he had vanished. 'Have you seen him anywhere down here? Walking beside the river?'

'Sorry, Mr Rhea,' said one of them. 'We've had our heads down, I'm afraid, we're after that big salmon they say is hereabouts ... in yon muddy pool, we think t'biggest that's been seen in this beck for years ... but I can't say we've noticed anybody since we arrived. That would be early, half-seven this morning or thereabouts. Not that we can see much from down here, not behind us on the cricket field, that is.'

'Thanks,' I said, adding, 'if you do see him when I've gone, tell him to get himself home, folks are out looking for him!'

'Right, we'll do that,' he assured me.

I moved on. The cricketers had a pitch in the centre of that large field and it was protected from the cattle by an electric fence. The outer field was the preserve of the cows which meant that the sound of a cricket ball plopping into a cowclap instead of running smoothly across the boundary for four runs had long been a part of

Aidensfield's cricketing lore. Some said it should count as six. Being a Wednesday, however, there was no match and the cows were present but unable to contaminate the pitch itself, and Glyn did not seem perturbed by them. He ran and fussed about the outer field, exploring mole hills, sniffing with his head down and eventually heading for a patch of gorse bushes and bracken on the elevated north-eastern corner.

I saw his stance change to one of alertness, his tail began to wag vigorously and then he barked. He rushed forwards towards the bushes and vanished into their thorny depths, tail wagging and barking with excitement. I waited for a few seconds, wondering what he would do next, but he didn't emerge and so it was time for me to examine those same bushes. I felt sure I would find Craig – and I did. He was sitting there in a cosy hide fashioned from the tall, thick bracken, but safely concealed by the thorny gorse, known hereabouts as whin. It was a very efficient hiding place, the sort in which some birds, such as linnets, build their nests. Without the dog, I would not have found him.

'Craig!' I called, as he tried to conceal himself by lying deeper in the bracken.

'Come along, it's time to go home.'

He lay as still as a rock for a few moments, then realized I had discovered him and, somewhat bashfully, he emerged with Glyn now jumping up and down and trying to lick his hands. He was clutching his satchel, empty because he'd eaten and drunk everything. He came towards me with his head bowed, as if expecting some kind of almighty telling-off.

'So, Craig, what's all this about?' I put to him. 'Hiding here all day, playing truant ... you've had us all very worried, your mum, Miss Preston, me.'

'Sorry, Mr Rhea,' he was on the verge of tears. 'I was going to go home soon, it's nearly home time.'

I glanced at my watch. It was twenty-past three.

'So you'd have gone home and pretended you'd been to school?'

He nodded.

'Your teacher told us.' I explained. 'They have to report to the authorities when a pupil doesn't arrive at school, just in case something seriously wrong has happened.'

'I'm sorry, Mr Rhea, I didn't know there'd be a fuss about me ... honest I didn't...'

'So, between you and me, as two fellers

talking together, why did you run away?'

'Run away? Oh, I didn't run away, Mr Rhea. I came to guard the kingfisher, to stop them catching it.'

'To stop who catching it?'

'Those two men.' I realized he was referring to the fishermen. From this slightly elevated vantage point, I could just see the tops of the heads of the two men as they continued their silent vigil beside the water.

'I don't understand.' He was now at my side, quite composed with his earlier signs of fear evaporating. 'What made you think those two men were going to catch the kingfisher? And which kingfisher are we talking about?'

'That one with a nest in the bank over there,' and he pointed across the field towards the northern-east tip of the field. 'They dig a tunnel into the bank, Mr Rhea, and lay their eggs really deep inside. They've got a nest there now. I've seen them coming and going ... I've been watching them. The young ones will be hatching soon. You can see the entrance if you stand on the bank under that oak tree.'

He pointed to the tree.

'Right,' I acknowledged. 'So you're looking after the kingfisher?'

'Yes. My dad says kingfishers are getting rarer, Mr Rhea, and I didn't want anybody to come and harm this one, or take its eggs, when those men said they were coming here today to catch it, I thought I'd better come and stop them.'

'And have they caught it?' I asked, not really believing that country people like these fishermen would harm such a nest. 'Or done anything to the nest?'

'No, Mr Rhea, they haven't. They've been sat there all day, just fishing.'

'With you watching them?'

He nodded.

I pondered this rather odd situation, not wishing to leave the scene until I had resolved it. Clearly, young Craig had some deep reason for watching those men all day – and uncharacteristically taking time off school to do so – and I wondered how or why he had come to such a conclusion about apparently innocent fishermen. And then I had the spark of an idea; it was based on something one of those lads had told me a few minutes earlier.

'Come with me,' I said to Craig, and then I walked towards the fishermen with Craig and his dog following. They heard our arrival and turned with a smile.

'Hello again,' I greeted them. 'Can I interrupt your mission for a moment?'

'We've got rod licences for salmon if that's what you're going to ask,' said the one who'd spoken to me earlier. 'I see you've found him, then?'

'Fortunately, yes,' I told them. 'This is Craig, the lad we've been looking for. Now I've something to ask you because he's been watching you all day. From those bushes behind me.'

'Watching us? What for?'

'He thought you were going to catch a kingfisher that's nesting a few yards up-river from you.'

'Aye, we saw the nest, that's one reason we're down here on this stretch, round the corner and out of sight of the birds. We don't want to disturb them.'

'So why did you think these men were going to catch the kingfisher?' I asked Craig.

'I heard them saying they were going to, at the cricket match on Saturday. I was there with my dad.' I knew that Aidensfield's opponents on Saturday had been Elsinby, and this pair had been members of the Elsinby team.

'Never!' cried one of the men. 'We never said anything of the sort!'

'Yes you did,' and Craig now burst into a fit of anger. 'You said you were coming down here to the cricket field on Wednesday to catch the kingfisher ... I heard you.'

'Hang on, Craig,' I placed an arm around his shoulders. 'Let's sort this out slowly, shall we?' I turned to the fishermen, asking, During the cricket match, did you say you were coming here today? Down to this part of the river? To catch the salmon?'

'Yes, that's when we decided to come, me and Jim talked about it while we were waiting our turn to bat ... there was folks all around us at the time this lad must have heard us and misunderstood.'

'You said you were going to catch the kingfisher!' Craig now burst into tears. 'And I wanted to stop you.'

I didn't ask how he had intended to halt them if they had gone ahead with such a scheme, but I thought I now knew the reason for his defence of that beautiful bird.

I addressed the fishermen again. 'You said this was the biggest salmon seen around here for years?'

'Aye, it is, a giant among salmon. Others have had a touch but never landed him, so we thought we'd have a crack with rods, lines and spinners not with flies. Flies are no good just there, the water's too muddy. We took time off work so we could spend the whole day on the river.'

'And how did you describe the fish?' I asked.

'Ah!' The spokesman of the pair now realized the drift of my question. 'We called him the king fish, didn't we, Ron?'

Ron nodded. 'Aye, he is, the king of the salmon. King fish. That's what we call 'em when they're the biggest.'

'So you said you were planning to catch the king fish?' I smiled, and watched as young Craig listened in some disbelief.

'Aye, that's what we said,' nodded Ron. 'It was me who said that, I allus call the big 'uns king fish.'

'Not kingfisher?' I smiled.

'Nay, Mr Rhea, we'd never hurt a kingfisher.'

'Come along, Craig,' I said. 'You've some explaining to do. You can start at my police van. I'll show you how to use the radio so you can get a message to your mum to say you're safe and sound.'

'I'm sorry, Mr Rhea, if I've caused trouble.'

'No harm done,' called the fishermen whose name I did not know. 'No harm done, Craig, but we'll keep an eye on that kingfisher for you. No need to bunk off school to do that, not while we're bunking off work to catch the king fish!'

Chapter 9

One of the fascinations of English law is that events can occur which in the opinion of the general public are wrong, but for which no legal provision is specifically made. If the careful wording of our criminal law does not stipulate that an action is illegal, therefore, then it may not be punishable as an offence. One example is behaviour now known as 'stalking'. Until the Protection from Harassment Act 1997 became law, there was little that could be done to prevent the odd behaviour of individuals who harassed others by constantly following and watching them or sending them unwanted declarations of their love. However, a good standby piece of legislation was – and still is – the wonderful Justice of the Peace Act of 1361. This ancient statute authorizes a person to be bound over to be of good behaviour even if no specific crime or offence has been committed. The term 'good behaviour' is very wide ranging, but being 'bound over' does not rank as a conviction although if the subject of the order disobeys it by committing an offence or ignoring the order by repeating his or her folly, then he or she can be returned to court and penalized. Creation of this law was one of the marvels of medieval times and the fact that it is still widely used is adequate proof of ancient wisdom.

On the other hand, of course, the law has a habit of creating offences which the general public do not regard as wrong or unlawful. Examples could be shaking a carpet or mat in the street (except door mats which can be shaken before 8 a.m.); wantonly disturbing residents by ringing doorbells and knocking on any door; placing lines or cords across the street and hanging washing from them; leaving sewer covers off; fixing window boxes on the outer ledges of upper windows without securing them, or making slides on ice or snow in the street. All these offences, and more (the essence of which are causing nuisance, obstruction and annoyance to residents) are contained in section 28 of the Town Police Clauses Act of 1847 and although it only applies to urban areas where it has been adopted, it was in force during my time at Aidensfield – and continues to be so.

One example of the law not catering for all eventualities can be illustrated by the fact that it was impossible, until 1971, for a person to commit arson of a motor vehicle. The Malicious Damage Act of 1861, which remained in force until 1971, created the statutory offence of arson, although it had earlier been catered for by Common Law. Under Common Law, arson was committed if anyone wilfully and maliciously set fire to the dwelling house of another but the Malicious Damage Act extended the crime by adding things like churches, warehouses, shops, buildings used for trade, farming and manufacturing, stations, docks, harbours, public buildings, any other building not specifically mentioned including those under construction, crops of various kinds, mines, ships, arsenals, dockyards and even gorse, furze or peat. This is an abbreviated list but the Act in its entirety greatly broadened the crime of arson.

Motor vehicles, however, had not been invented at the time this Act was introduced and so, in later years, if anyone set fire to a car, lorry or bus, they could not be charged with arson. The exception might be if the vehicle was inside one of the buildings to which the crime of arson might be applied, but if someone set fire to the vehicle in the street or open air, the culprit could not be charged with arson.

Common sense prevailed, however. It was possible to charge the culprit with malicious damage! Since the passing of the Criminal Damage Act of 1971, the offence of criminal damage protects *any* property belonging to another, and if such property is deliberately burned, the offender can now be charged with arson – even if it is a motor car!

It follows there could be great fun studying the more unusual statutes, if only to be aware of them rather than hoping to put them into effect, but within the police service, we had always to be alert to the possibility of someone breaking one or other of the more unusual laws. In Aidensfield, if someone was going to break one of those laws, then it was almost sure to be Claude Jeremiah Greengrass – and so it transpired.

The problem began when he bought a dog cart at a sale of household goods in Elsinby. The original dog carts were made for transporting sporting dogs to shooting venues, but in time the term came to be used for a variety of small, light carts, even if they were drawn by horses. In some cases, carts were made tiny enough to be drawn by large dogs, but in the case of Claude's purchase, it was far too small to be hauled by something like a St Bernard or a mastiff. The general belief was that it was more of a toy than a genuine, serviceable vehicle, but it appeared to have been made for haulage by a pet dog, probably one belonging to a child. It had four wooden spoked wheels about the size of those on a pram and they were fitted with solid rubber tyres. The leading pair of wheels were on a turntable beneath the cart at the end of a pair of shafts like those of a horse-drawn cart, albeit far smaller. In the cart compartment there was a small seat located towards the rear.

This would not carry more than one small child. The whole contraption was made of wood and was thought to have been built during the 1850s or thereabouts. It was brightly coloured with red, green and cream paint and it was in excellent condition. Claude bought it for £3 10s. 0d. and bore it home in triumph. We all wondered what he would do with it; I thought he would try to re-sell it for a handsome profit in an antique shop or even the local saleroom.

Claude's purchase led to me being surprised some weeks later, when a lady hailed me as I walked, in uniform, along the street outside the Aidensfield Stores. She wanted to discuss some aspects of her teenage son's application for his first driving licence and I was happy to explain the procedures, then she mentioned Claude's new egg delivery service.

'Egg delivery service?' I smiled, wondering whether such a scheme would be financially worthwhile if he used his old lorry.

'Yes, with that little cart of his, pulled along by Alfred, his dog you know.'

'You mean that dog cart he bought at the sale the other week?'

'Yes,' she said. 'Alfred is so proud of it. He's got a special harness and he trots along with the cart behind. Claude fills it with boxes of eggs and they go from door to door, delivering orders. Everyone loves it and Alfred looks so cute. Some ladies have ordered a dozen eggs just to see Alfred trotting up their garden path with his cart.'

'I wouldn't have thought Alfred was reliable enough to be allowed to haul a loaded cart. Suppose he chases a cat or something?' I laughed.

'Oh, Claude says that when Alfred's between the shafts, he's as good as gold, he recognizes his responsibilities and behaves as well as any highly trained horse. Claude says he's not worried about Alfred racing off after cats and rabbits, not when he's hauling his cart.'

'I've not seen this phenomenon,' I admitted, and then, after completing our chat, she left to go along to the post office for a driver's licence application form for her son. From my point of view, my first instinct, knowing Claude Jeremiah, was that his enterprise must be the subject of some kind of legal stipulation. My early concern was whether or not he needed a licence of any kind. Did his activities bring him within the scope of a pedlar's certificate, for example, or did he need a hawker's licence? I racked my brains to recall my training school tuition on such characters.

A pedlar is a person who, *without* a horse or other beast bearing or drawing burden, travels and trades on foot and goes from town to town or to other men's houses, carrying to sell or exposing for sale any goods, wares or merchandise *immediately* to be delivered, or offering for sale his skill in handicraft. The essence of a pedlar's craft is that he travels on foot to sell his wares or skills. In thinking of Alfred and his cart, the dog might be considered a beast who was drawing burden, but in most other respects Claude fitted the definition of a pedlar. Certainly, if he was *not* accompanied by Alfred, as he trudged from house to house on foot selling merchandise, then Claude could be considered a pedlar. And if he was a pedlar, he needed a pedlar's certificate.

It seemed, however, that because Claude was accompanied by a beast who was drawing burden, he was more likely to be classified as a hawker. A hawker was a person who travelled with a horse or other beast bearing or drawing burden, and who went from place to place or to other men's houses carrying to sell, or exposing for sale any goods, wares or merchandise, *or* exposing samples or patterns of any goods, wares and merchandise to be *afterwards* delivered.

But could a dog be regarded as a beast, in particular, a beast of burden? It seemed that because Claude was accompanied by an animal who was drawing burden, and that his goods were carried for sale, he fitted the definition of a hawker. If he was a hawker, therefore, he needed a hawker's licence which he should obtain from the county council. In addition, he would need the words 'Licensed Hawker' to be painted on Alfred's dog cart, but then I remembered that a person who sells fish, fruit, victuals or coal does *not* need a hawker's licence. Eggs, I suppose, were classed as victuals... In any case, I began to wonder whether anyone would seriously regard Alfred as a beast of burden – it was not as if he was a mule or an elephant. These memories from my training school flooded my mind as I walked along the main street, and at this point I popped into the post office to buy a postal order.

The moment Oscar Blaketon spotted me, he said, 'Ah, Nick, just the fellow. Greengrass! You'll have to do something about that man!'

'Why? What's he done now?' I smiled.

'You've seen that contraption of his, have you? That cart with Alfred between the shafts? If that daft dog takes off after a cat or something, just when there's a car or motor bike passing, there could be nasty accident.'

'I've heard about the dog cart, Oscar, but haven't seen it in action yet. I saw it when he bought it as I was on duty at the auction, but his new door-to-door service has yet to reveal itself to me. I don't think he's called at the police house with his eggs.'

'He wouldn't, would he? He's breaking the law, I suppose you realize that?' said Blaketon with just a hint of his former career showing through his thin smile.

'If it's licences you're thinking about, I don't think he falls into the category of either a pedlar or a hawker,' I began. 'And I'm not sure Alfred is a beast of burden...'

'I'm not talking about that. It's illegal, Nick, having a cart which is drawn by a dog on a public highway.'

'I thought dog carts were made especially for them to do that? I'm sure I've seen pictures of big dogs like mastiffs pulling carts along.'

'On private land perhaps, and in the grounds of country estates, but not on the public highway, Nick. The gentry might have done that in the past, but now it's considered cruel – section 9 of the Protection of Animals Act, 1911, if my memory serves me. It's along the lines that it is illegal to use, cause, procure, or, being the owner, to permit to be used, any dog for the purpose of drawing or helping to draw any cart or truck on any public highway. So there you are, chapter and verse from the deepest recesses of memory. You'll have to report him for summons, Nick.'

'I'll see to it,' I assured him.

Back in my office, I checked Moriarty's *Police Law* and found that Oscar Blaketon was correct. By using Alfred to haul a cart on a public road, Claude was breaking the law and so I would acquaint him, and tell him to end the practice. I would not take him to court, unless of course, he persisted after that first warning.

As things transpired, there was no need even to warn Claude because Alfred, on duty the very next day while hauling his cart full of cartons of fresh eggs, allowed his poacher's dog instincts to get the better of him when he spotted a hare. Unable to resist the challenge, he galloped after the hare which soon took evasive action by leaping across a ditch and bolting through a hedge into a field. Alfred tried to follow but the cart overturned in the ditch and went no further, and even though Alfred managed to struggle free from his harness to force his way through the hedge, he was too late to catch the relieved hare. Claude's load of eggs, about ten dozen in all, was transformed into a raw omelette much to the delight of some local flies, other creepy-crawlies and some little wild beasts of the hedgerow, thus Alfred's career as a beast of burden came to an abrupt end.

I cannot say I was sorry.

Although criminal law provides for lots of offences relating to drunkenness, there is no legal definition of this condition, although, like a giraffe, most of us recognize it when we see it.

It is that blissful state which exists when a person has consumed alcohol in quantities which can produce a reduction in the ability to control one's faculties, but for a person who never drinks alcohol, the enjoyment of just one schooner of sherry might achieve that result. At the other end of the boozing scale, some people can consume oceans of alcoholic beverage without any apparent ill effect. It is probably for this reason that the law has never attempted to define drunkenness or to regulate the amount we can legally drink, although it does seek to rationalize our more obnoxious behaviour by creating a range of offences in which drunkenness is a key factor.

These vary from simple drunkenness to the offence of being drunk and incapable, the latter being a state where one is unable to care for oneself. One can be drunk and disorderly, drunk in charge of a loaded firearm, drunk in charge of a child under seven years of age, drunk in charge of a steam engine and drunk in charge of a hackney carriage. There are offences of being drunk on a passenger steamer, drunk on licensed premises, riding a bicycle while drunk and being drunk in charge of a carriage (and a bicycle is a carriage for this purpose), and of course, driving a motor vehicle while under the influence of drink or drugs, or with more than the prescribed limit of alcohol in the bloodstream.

One effective way of dealing with male drunks out of court was to place them in a taxi and send them home to their wives or mothers – the cost of the fare (usually inflated by the cabby) was often sufficient punishment, to say nothing of the subsequent tongue-lashing from the lady of the house.

Where possible, the police avoid the trouble of prosecuting drunks in court unless, of course, their behaviour deserves a sharp lesson, or they had done something unreasonable or harmful while under the influence of alcohol. But with a chap wending his merry way home, singing softly to himself and staggering mildly while causing no trouble, to anyone, the police would invariably adopt the gentle and sympathetic approach.

It was recalling the need for such discretion, so essential in police work, that I wondered what to do about Amos Spooner. Amos was a long-haired, whiskery itinerant farm worker who was always accompanied by his black-and-white cur, Ben. Unmarried, Amos rented a cottage from the landlord of the Hopbind Inn at Elsinby. A stone-built but rather tumbledown shack, it was along a lane some fifty yards from the pub, almost out of sight from the village. Nonetheless, this was a happy and convenient location due to Amos's regular and essential visits to the hostelry.

In his mid-fifties, Amos worked on a day-to-day basis, hiring himself to farmers, landowners and estate managers and he undertook every possible task expected of a general labourer. He cleared ditches, cut hedges, tended cattle, sheep and pigs, helped with the harvest and hay-time, picked potatoes, milked cattle, clipped sheep and even painted buildings, cleared drains, spread muck, weeded among turnips and fixed roofing tiles. For the farmers of the district, Amos was a very useful character because he never expected to be employed full-time and most of the payments he received were in cash or even kind, such as eggs, milk, potatoes, meat and firewood.

I have no idea how he coped with official-dom such as National Insurance or the Inland Revenue, but he always had enough cash in his pockets to pay his rent and rates, eat well (often in the pub) and enjoy most evenings in the bar of the Hopbind. He could be seen there some lunchtimes too, especially when he was not working. Those requiring his assistance, sometimes at very short notice, knew where to find him.

The frequency of his visits to the Hopbind Inn, and the fact he had few major expenses to worry about, meant that he spent his money freely on beer and in turn, he was thus often in a very mellow or even merry condition upon leaving the premises. No one complained about him because he rarely ventured into the village centre in that condition; more often than not, he simply left the pub, turned left and made for home, singing gently to himself as he staggered along the leafy lane. He was never violent, abusive or objectionable.

Much of Amos's work came from his close association with the Hopbind. He did not have a telephone so farmers wishing to offer him a few days' or a few weeks' work knew they could always find him in the bar. They'd find an excuse to pop in for a chat with Amos and inevitably, they also bought drinks or even food, and thus Amos was a treasured asset to financial well-being of that establishment. Not surprisingly, the landlord would provide him with free beer and food if he was short of cash and so, for all sorts of reasons, it was a most amicable arrangement.

For all that, it never occurred to me that, one day, I might have to consider arresting Amos for drunkenness for neither I, nor anyone who knew him, regarded his conduct as that of a drunkard. It is true that he was often very merry and blissfully happy due to the quantity of drink he had consumed, but he was never a nuisance to anyone and certainly he did not wander around the village with loaded shotguns, children under the age of seven or steam engines.

It was perhaps unfortunate, therefore, that Sergeant Craddock decided to join me in an official tour of the pubs on my patch on the very day that Amos found himself being offered an opportunity to perform a small task. Amos and Ben, his dog, had arrived at the Hopbind Inn around twelve noon where Amos ordered his usual pint, along with a large pork pie, pickled egg and packet of potato crisps. He ordered two small pies for Ben. Having enjoyed the first pint, he ordered a second, with another pickled egg, and then a third pint. It was at this point that Herbert Grantley, who farmed at Low Mires on the outskirts of Elsinby, happened to arrive, hoping to find Amos in the bar. And he bought Amos his fourth pint and allowed Amos to return the favour while buying himself a fifth.

'Ah've a small job for thoo,' Herbert had said. 'Cash in hand.'

'When?' asked Amos.

'Now,' said Herbert, qualifying that by adding, 'Well, Ah mean, when thoo's finished thi dinner. That's if thoo's nut fixed up wi' summat else.'

'Nay,' Amos had said. 'Ah've nowt on and Ah can deea wiv a spot o' cash. So what's thoo gitten in mind?'

Herbert had a field containing fifty-five ewes and because they'd eaten most of the grass, he felt it was time to transfer them to pastures new. The field where they now reclined was one he had rented, and it lay along Ploatby Lane almost a mile from his own premises. All he wanted was for Amos and his dog to fetch the sheep from that distant field and return them to Ten Acre, a field on his own farm with a rich supply of fresh new grass. The route was straightforward because it was along a surfaced lane which provided a direct link between the two fields. Amos agreed – it was a simple task and he could do the job immediately after closing time and so earn himself a small fee. That would pay for this evening's beer and a chicken-in-a-basket. Herbert bought another round of pints and said he'd give Amos and Ben a lift to the field when the pub closed; it would take Amos not more than half-an-hour to round up the animals and complete his task.

In Ashfordly Section car, Craddock and I arrived at the Hopbind just after it had closed for the afternoon. Amos and Herbert had already left and the premises were empty, thus giving us an opportunity for a quiet talk with George Ward, the landlord. George was cousin of the other George Ward, landlord of the Brewers Arms at Aidensfield, a fact which sometimes caused confusion. Craddock wanted a general talk about enforcement of the licensing laws particularly so far as they affected young people, adding we had no reason to complain about the conduct of this inn and its customers. It was friendly and affable aimed at establishing uniformity of conduct throughout the licensed premises within Ashfordly Section, and as we talked, we enjoyed a coffee with George, and then departed.

Our intended destination was Slemmington, where the Golden Globe, a licensed restaurant with a growing reputation for quality, had recently opened, and we decided to travel along the back roads through Ploatby and Thackerston. As we rounded a bend in Ploatby Lane, we were confronted by a flock of sheep completely blocking the road; they were heading towards us with Amos at the rear and Ben performing beautifully as a highly skilled sheepdog. In normal circumstances, all a motorist can do in such a case is to halt the vehicle and wait until all the sheep have passed. But Amos did not seem to realize that we had arrived because he was waving his arms around as if he was conducting an orchestra and his head was thrown back and moving in conjunction with his arms. When I lowered the window, I could hear the tuneless strains of 'Land of Hope and Glory'. Ben seemed in control of the sheep because Amos was at least fifty yards behind them, totally oblivious to what was happening. He was completely absorbed by his solo per-formance although he broke off occasionally to give orders to Ben.

'What on earth is that man doing?' Crad-dock asked.

'Singing,' I said, adding, 'Perhaps the sheep like music...'

'I wouldn't call that music, PC Rhea! I could get a better tune out of a comb and paper! You know what I think? I think, he's drunk!'

We had now come to a standstill and were prepared to wait as the sheep milled around us to continue their journey, but Craddock was now leaning his head out of the window and staring at Amos. 'He is drunk, PC Rhea. That man is definitely drunk!'

'Merry, I'd say.' I was familiar with Amos's routine. 'He's not incapable and he's not disorderly. There's no one here but those sheep–'

'And us! We are here, PC Rhea, and we represent the law. Some courts might accept that singing "Land of Hope and Glory" to a flock of sheep in the middle of the road is a form of disorderliness ... so, you need to take action, PC Rhea. I shall prosecute that man as an example to others. After all, we are on a mission to review our enforcement of the liquor licensing laws and this is a blatant breach. So, out you get. Arrest him, put him in the car and we will take him to Ashfordly Police Station immediately.'

'What about the sheep?' I asked.

'Put them in the nearest field,' he snapped. 'That one over there, with sheep in it.'

'We can't do that, Sergeant. One must never mix animals like that; how could one farmer identify his own flock from the others? And if we use another field, there might be disease, poison on the ground, all sorts of problems. We can't just get rid of sheep like that. Besides, the Force could be faced with a claim for damages and I don't think the chief constable would be too happy about that.'

'We cannot let an offence like this go un-challenged, PC Rhea. He is breaking the law.'

'Is he?'

'Yes, PC Rhea. He is drunk in charge of sheep on the public highway. That is a criminal offence under section 12 of the Licensing Act of 1872 – it includes being drunk in charge of a horse, cattle, pigs, as well as a carriage and a steam engine.'

'Not all at the same time, I trust!' I smiled at him.

'Don't be facetious, PC Rhea!'

'Well, Sergeant, if he is drunk and we let him continue,' I said, tongue in cheek, 'we'll be aiding and abetting his offence, won't we? So does that mean I have to get out of the car and shepherd those sheep myself?'

'You are making unnecessary difficulties, PC Rhea,' he snapped.

'Sergeant,' I said, 'I have to live in this community with these people and if I report Amos for being drunk in charge of a flock of sheep, I shall be the laughing stock of the area, and so will the entire police service.'

'We do not make the laws, PC Rhea, that is done by Parliament. Our job is to enforce them without fear or favour. If that man has committed an offence, then it is our duty to report the matter and let the court decide what action to take. Out you get, make the necessary assessment of his condition and if necessary, report him. I am a witness if you need one. Now, you should take responsibility for those sheep and drive them to wherever they are going. I shall expect an offence report on my desk within the week!'

The sheep were now running past our car with Ben darting backwards and forwards, driving them, rounding up strays, keeping them in a neat bunch and doing all the work. I waited until they were clear of the car and got out. Craddock drove off leaving me stranded in the lane with Amos heading towards me, still conducting his invisible orchestra.

'Now then, Constable Rhea,' he beamed when he saw me. 'Is yon chap your boss?'

'He is, that's Sergeant Craddock,' I told him.

'He leeaks a bit of a sour face ti me,' he smiled. 'Didn't he like being held up?'

'He thinks you are drunk,' I said.

'Nay, lad, not me. Ah wouldn't be here if Ah was drunk, would Ah? Ah'd be laid flat on my back somewhere, fast asleep and snoring my head off.'

'So where are you taking these sheep?'

'Herbert Grantley's Ten Acre,' he said. 'Ah've oppened gate riddy for 'em, Ah did that afore Ah came down this way, and Ben saw me do it. He knows where to tak 'em, Ah've no need to say owt to 'im. He's in charge of them ewes, not me. He'll run 'em right along to Herbert's gate and turn 'em into his field, clean as a whistle. There's neea need for me ti deea owt, really.'

'Thanks,' I said. 'That's all I need to know. Mind if I keep you company? My sergeant's gone off and left me!'

'Please yourself,' he grinned. 'But Ah'll not inflict my singing on you, but Ah do like yon Elgar chap, 'Land of Hope and Glory' and all that ... good stuff, it is.'

He was chatting to me with no sign of drunkenness or slurred words, and I was aware he'd had the foresight to open the field gate in advance to admit the incoming sheep; those were not the actions of a drunk. I walked beside him as Ben drove the flock ahead of us and soon I saw him dart ahead and stand in the road at the far side of the open gate. The lead ewe saw him and turned into the field and, as sheep do, the rest followed her. Ben remained near the gate until we reached it, then Amos closed it.

'There we are, Constable Rhea, another good job done. Not a bad day's work.'

That excursion meant I had to walk home from Elsinby, two miles or so, but I did not mind because it was a lovely day, but within ten minutes of me returning home, the telephone rang. It was Sergeant Craddock.

'Ah, PC Rhea, you got home then?'

'Yes, Sergeant. No problems.'

'Now, I am in the inspector's office at Eltering and want to discuss this business about those sheep–'

'Sergeant, I talked to Amos and there was no sign of drunkenness in him, his speech was not slurred, he was steady on his feet but he was singing and conducting because he happens to like Elgar ... and...' I paused.

'Go on, PC Rhea.'

'He was not in charge of those sheep. The dog was. I watched it at work; Amos had opened the field gate a mile ahead and the dog knew exactly what to do ... and I know of no offence of being drunk in charge of a sheepdog.'

'Clearly you have made a rational assessment of the situation, but I have also been giving thought to this matter and I agree that it would be very bad public relations to report such an incident for prosecution. So, tear up your report, will you?'

'Yes, Sergeant,' I smiled. He was not to know I had not written any such report but I let him think he had made a good decision, although I wondered whether the fact that he was currently in the inspector's office had any bearing on his change of mind. I happened to know that the inspector also liked Elgar's music.

Chapter 10

It was a chilly autumn Saturday, with more than a hint of snow in the air, and I had completed my first four hours of duty. I had climbed out of bed at quarter past five so that I could have some breakfast and prepare myself for a dawn patrol beginning at 6 a.m. and finishing at 10 a.m. For half of that day's hours of patrolling, therefore, I had driven and walked around my patch mostly in darkness, checking shops, explosives' stores and other vulnerable properties to see if there'd been any overnight break-ins while keeping an eye open for early-morning poachers. That part of my duty completed, I had the middle of the day to myself.

I had to remain available, however, because I was on call, with a further four-hour patrol scheduled for later, i.e. 8 p.m. until midnight. That would complete my eight hours' official work. It was a long day, with my duty time spread across nineteen hours but it was necessary because there was a dance in the village hall at which my presence was required. Provided I was not called out to an emergency of any kind, or to deal with a traffic accident, I could relax a little.

Mary had taken the children to visit their grandmother and, as part of her new part-time job, Mary had some cosmetics to deliver en route, but I had to be available for duty, albeit spending the time at home. To occupy myself, I decided to tidy the garden for the final time this year – I had to trim the beech hedge and give the lawn its final cut of the season before cleaning the grasscutter and putting my gardening tools in storage for the winter.

Having eaten a hearty late second break-fast, I changed into my gardening clothes and began my horticultural chores. It would be about noon when I heard the telephone ringing in my office and, after a brisk sprint up the garden, I managed to reach it before it stopped. Panting heavily and anticipating some kind of call-out, I gasped, 'Aidensfield Police.'

'Ah, Nick.' I recognized the distinctive sound of Oscar Blaketon's voice. 'Glad I caught you. I thought you might be out, seeing you didn't answer for a while.'

'I was down the garden,' I told him. 'So what can I do for you?'

'I'd like a word with you,' he said. 'I wondered about a pint and a steak pie or something at the Aidensfield pub? After I close for the afternoon?'

'I'm on call,' I told him. 'I'm working late tonight, and I've got to be handy for the phone during the day, just in case.'

'Well, you can leave the house, you know, so long as you provide a contact number. So how about it? One o'clock in the bar?'

'Well, thanks, yes. I'm alone today, Mary's gone off with the children, so it'll be nice to have lunch out. I'll ring Ashfordly Police Station and tell them where I can be contacted.'

'Good, I'll see you there.'

At one o'clock, with my gardening clothing discarded and now dressed in slacks and a sweater, I entered the bar to find it filled with noise and chatter, with Blaketon buying drinks for about twenty people, all men. I spotted Alf Ventress among the crowd.

Blaketon spotted me and beckoned me to join them and, as I went across, he handed me a pint of bitter and said, 'The drinks are on me, Nick, and lunch too. We're all having steak pie, chips and peas...'

'Fine!' I was surprised to be included in this unexpected gathering. 'So what's it all about? Is it your birthday?'

'More important than that. I've got that small back room reserved for us when we eat. All at very short notice, but I like to spring surprises ... drink up.'

'I can't have too much, not if I might be called out.'

'Fair enough, you know the routine, but don't be frightened to enjoy yourself. There's a good range of soft drinks, don't forget. All on me.'

And so I joined in the merriment, not really knowing why I had been summoned at such short notice. I chatted to Alf and some of the others, all of whom were equally puzzled and then George Ward, the landlord, announced, 'It's ready through the back, Oscar. Steak pie, chips and peas, twenty times. It's on the table now.'

Like a party of schoolchildren, we formed a procession and made our way into the back room where a log fire was burning and the table was set with twenty places each bearing a plate of hot steak pie, chips and peas, providing a lovely scented and highly appetizing welcome. Blaketon made sure we all had a drink as we took our places, and I made sure I was seated next to Alf. That way, I'd have someone to talk to. I think most of the other guests were Blaketon's golfing friends or some of his acquaintances from Ashfordly. I recognized a local solicitor among them.

Once we were settled, Blaketon stood up and rapped a spoon on the table as he called for silence and so we all stopped talking to gaze at him.

'Before we eat,' he said, 'I want to say just a few words. I'm pleased you can all join me at this extremely short notice but it is a rather special occasion. This is a celebration of sorts, the first of several I hope, but this morning I felt I wanted to share my good news with people whom I regard as rather special to me, people who in recent weeks have helped me more than they realize. All I want to say to you all is that I am now the owner of this establishment – this pub is mine, gentlemen, lock, stock and barrel. The deal was confirmed this very morning; George will be retiring at the end of the month when I shall be moving into the premises. Gina will remain, I shall be owner of the inn, but not the licensee – that will be Gina.'

Someone shouted, 'Three cheers for

Oscar Blaketon,' and we all stood up to drink his health.

He smiled and blushed somewhat, adding, 'I just want to say that the post office business will be sold, so this will be my new future, gentlemen, and this is my way of conveying an early thank you to each of you. In one way or another, you've all helped me to reach this decision, and you've kept my negotiations a secret as I asked. So thank you, all of you. Now it's in the open and I must say I am relieved!'

We cheered him and he looked rather moved by the reception we gave him. He told us there would be a larger and more formal celebration once he was settled in, but this was a quick means of simultaneously announcing his good news. There was a good deal of light-hearted banter about parties in pubs, barmaids and coppers, and then, as the initial excitement subsided, Alf Ventress turned to address me. 'Did you know about this, Nick? That Oscar was buying this place?'

'I knew he was interested,' I admitted. 'He talked it over with me, on the quiet.'

'Me too,' he smiled. 'I thought it was a good idea; he needs something that's more of a challenge than retirement … so yes, I said he should go ahead, he's got a few years in him yet. But it might not be easy for you, having your former sergeant running a pub on your patch!'

'I don't think he'll cause me problems.' I tried to sound confident. 'But let's face it, Alf, I might leave here before he retires next time round. I won't be at Aidensfield for ever, you know.'

'Don't tell me you're leaving as well!' He sounded shocked.

'I've no plans to leave Aidensfield, Alf,' I tried to assure him. 'I'm just reminding myself, I suppose, that country coppers tend to move on after five years or so.'

'Have you been asked about a move, then? By the powers-that-be? Have they been putting feelers out, asking if you'd be prepared to transfer somewhere?'

'No, they haven't, Alf,' and I tried to sound convincing.

'But you have passed your exams, haven't you? And you have appeared before the promotion board, so it wouldn't surprise me if we see you heading for great things before too long. Like Oscar Blaketon, you've got to move on, Nick.'

'I can't say I'd want a pub, though!' I laughed.

'Me neither, it's too much like hard work,' Alf chuckled, as he tucked into his steak pie.

That evening, as I began my four-hour patrol at eight o'clock, my first task was to motor into Ashfordly where I popped into the police station to deliver some reports and collect any internal mail from my docket. Awaiting me was a small brown envelope which looked very official – my name was typed on the front – 'PC Rhea, Aidensfield.'

I opened it. It was a memo from the chief constable and it said, *'PC Rhea. This is to inform you that your interview by the promotion board was successful. This has been noted on your personal record.'*

And that was it.

The key to my own future now rested firmly with me and I knew that I must address the distinct possibility that I could soon be leaving Aidensfield.

The publishers hope that this book has given you enjoyable reading. Large Print Books are especially designed to be as easy to see and hold as possible. If you wish a complete list of our books please ask at your local library or write directly to:

Magna Large Print Books
Magna House, Long Preston,
Skipton, North Yorkshire.
BD23 4ND